Steele

P9-CQD-814

Pippa Passes

BY THE SAME AUTHOR

RUMER GODDEN

Pippa
Passes

William Morrow and Company, Inc.
New York

Copyright © 1994 by Rumer Godden

First published in Great Britain in 1994 by Macmillan, London

All rights reserved. No part of this book may be reproduced or utilized in any form
or by any means, electronic or mechanical, including photocopying, recording, or
by any information storage or retrieval system, without permission in writing from the
Publisher. Inquiries should be addressed to Permissions Department, William Morrow
and Company, Inc., 1350 Avenue of the Americas, New York, N.Y. 10019.

It is the policy of William Morrow and Company, Inc., and its imprints and affiliates,
recognizing the importance of preserving what has been written, to print the books
we publish on acid-free paper, and we exert our best efforts to that end.

Library of Congress Cataloging-in-Publication Data

Godden, Rumer, 1907–
Pippa passes / Rumer Godden.
p. cm.
ISBN 0-688-13397-5
1. British—Travel—Italy—Venice—Fiction. 2. Ballet dancers—Italy—Venice—
Fiction. 3. Young women—Italy—Venice—Fiction.
4. Venice (Italy)—Fiction. I. Title..
PR6013.02P5 1994   94-18336
823'
.912—dc20   CIP

Printed in the United States of America

First U. S. Edition

1 2 3 4 5 6 7 8 9 10

To E. Temple Thurston in gratitude for the book
that Pippa – and I – read.

From *Pippa Passes*

The year's at the spring
And day's at the morn;
Morning's at seven;
The hill-side's dew-pearled;
The lark's on the wing;
The snail's on the thorn;
God's in his heaven –
All's right with the world!

But . . .

Robert Browning

ACKNOWLEDGEMENTS

My grateful thanks to: Miss Pauline Wadsworth, M.R.A.D., teacher and senior ballet mistress at the Royal Ballet School, Whitelodge, Richmond, for her invaluable help on matters of a ballet company on a continental tour: to Michael Gluck-stern, British Consul in Venice, who smoothed my path in every possible way, and to Patricia Weston Liane, interpreter and Location Unit Manager, for her tireless and sympathetic Venetian research: travellers to the city will not find the Palazzetto dell'Orlando, nor the little church of San Giuseppe with its filigree tree in its square but there are many like them. Thank you, too, Franco, our gondolier, and Mrs Peggy McKeener, who has been with me throughout this work.

Then I must thank Ian Holmes of 'Music' Dumfries for his instructing me about the band; as always Sheila Anderson for her inexhaustible patience in typing and retyping - she has a genius for deciphering my handwriting; Hazel Orme who edited the book with such sensitivity, and Honi Werner for her beautiful and evocative jacket. Above all, and again as always, I thank Alan Maclean for his reading and guidance over the book.

—R.G.

A FOREWORD

It seems, for travellers nowadays, there are two Venices, both extreme – she is not a city of mediocrity. For many, her strange rich history, her treasures, the beauty of her churches, palaces, tall houses with their blending colours, the fascination of her waterways are overlaid by the decay, stale smells and filth, with the overpress of tourists, extortionate prices, the unfriendliness – I should say reserve – of her inhabitants unless you have money. These poor visitors do not even notice the famous, ever-changing translucent Venetian light; her magic is not for them.

Others, perhaps now only a few, are captivated. Long after they leave they will remember that light; remember, too, hidden canals with gardens and houses which tourists seldom see – the canals are too narrow for the *vaporetti*, water ferries, to use and gondolas are ludicrously expensive. I would, though, sacrifice a great deal to go in a gondola, particularly at night when one can hear the lapping of the water round the boat, the gondolier's cry of '*Ohé*' as he rounds the corners. They will remember churches, big and little, the great piazza San Marco with its winged lion on its pillar, the pigeons, the café music and other small, tucked-away *campielli* and squares, the markets – and the romance.

By good fortune I had had my eyes opened to Venice long before I saw her.

I must have been in my late teens when, in one of the second-hand bookshops I haunted in the Sussex town where I was born, I picked up a book, heavy, bound in green cloth, lettered in gold. It was by E. Temple

Thurston of whom I had never heard but he was evidently a well-known writer. Published in 1909, this book had had several editions, as had his other novels listed on the first page; it had kept its value, second hand, and three decades later it cost five pounds, in those days quite a sum.

The book was illustrated in black and white with many full-page illustrations which I did not like – they were mostly of people not well drawn. What immediately caught me were the small sketches in the margins, sketches of a water city I had dimly known of but had not visualized. Here were domes, towers, pinnacles, arches, stone bridges, small stone-flagged alleyways – it seemed there was not one spacious street; glimpses of canals, big and little with boats, endless boats, barges, many of them long, graceful, elongated craft steered by a man standing on the stern with a single oar; sketches of markets on the canal banks, of a wide lagoon. All far removed from anything I had seen.

I bought the book and read it; even then I recognized how unashamedly sentimental it was – novels were sentimental at the turn of the century and this was a love story – but, in spite of that, its evocation of Venice cast such a spell that it has been with me ever since. Though I fully admit the truths of her detractors, I feel that spell again every time I go there, not just the spell of her riches but of Venice herself – unique, Venice *serenissima*, and I yield myself to her.

'But you are not a sensible person,' people say to me.

They are probably right, though I like to think I am. Yet one thing I do know: there is a sense that goes beyond the practical and I am grateful that it has been vouchsafed to me. Sensible people, I suppose, would trade a Titian or the Teotoca Madonna of Torcello for an improvement in the drainage system – badly needed – but drains can be replaced; Titian's Assumption and the eight-hundred-year-old Madonna with tears on her cheeks as she weeps over the perversity of humans – never.

R.G.

PROLOGUE

'May I have your attention, everyone?'

The Company of the Midland Cities Ballet had arrived in Venice that Sunday afternoon for the first step of its Italian tour and Angharad Fullerton, its ballet mistress, had come to the Pensione Benvenuto where the *corps* were staying to brief them. For some reason, the Company manager had booked the men separately: 'Well, there isn't room for all of you here,' Angharad had excused him but the girls, especially, were discontented; Anne Marie and Dermot who had been together for two years immediately moved out and made their own arrangements. 'But I advise you to stay,' Angharad said now. 'Venice is full and you will be so busy you'll hardly notice.'

She went on: 'Tomorrow, Monday, class at ten thirty in the studio of the Teatro La Fenice, the opera house. Robert will still be setting the stage' – Robert Roberts was the stage manager. 'Class followed by rehearsal, in the rehearsal room which will probably run into the afternoon. Tuesday, the same but rehearsal will be on stage, evening calls possible. Wednesday evening is our première so morning class, rehearsal until two or thereabouts, warm-up class at six, performance eight. Following days are the same except that on Saturday and the Wednesday and Saturday after, there will be matinées at five. Here are copies of a map to show you how to get to the Fenice; you can walk there easily over the Accademia bridge.'

Her glance went over them: Pearl, Constance, Juliet, Anne Marie, Zoë, Jenny and fourteen more, twenty in all, who with fifteen young men made up the *corps*; last of all was Pippa Fane, youngest and newly joined. 'I don't want to dictate,' said Angharad, 'but some of you may not have been abroad before, I don't think any of you to Venice.' The glance rested for a moment on Pippa; it was certainly a first time for her, first of many if she, Angharad, had her way, and she meant to have her way.

'Venice is a romantic and fascinating city full of treasures – I hope it can be arranged for you to see some of them – but it is only too easy here to be distracted and, I needn't remind you, you are here to dance. And it has a bad reputation, so a word to you all. Italian men are notorious.'

'Really!' whispered Pearl in expostulation – she was one of the older dancers and the leader of the *corps*. 'My sister and I went all over Italy by ourselves when we were sixteen.'

'You mean we might pick a young man up or be picked up on the piazza San Marco?' Juliet was bolder with Angharad than the others. 'You tempt me', but Angharad was unperturbed.

'Exactly, so don't go about alone. Keep together. Don't get drawn into conversations. They'll try and chat you up.'

'Italians don't,' murmured Constance, who was also travelled.

'Take the *vaporetti*, the steam ferries. Don't be inveigled into clubbing together to take gondolas.' The girls glanced at one another, slightly guilty.

'There is an English dance company come for a season at La Fenice,' Nicolò, the young gondolier, told his mother.

'How do you know?'

'I brought some of the *signorine* from the station to their *pensione*.'

'*Subrettine*! Show girls!' said Leda. 'Pah!'

I

For Pippa it had begun in England two months before. She had been sitting on the floor after class in one of the ballet's studios, putting away her *pointe* shoes, carefully winding their ribbons, now and then stopping to wipe her face with her towel – she was hot and sweating – when Callum, one of the Company's first soloists, put his head round the door.

'Pippa, Humphrey wants you in his office.'

'Mr Blair!' She was still in such awe of the Company's hierarchy that she had not dared to call them by first names and Humphrey Blair was director and chief of the whole Midland Cities Ballet. 'Oh, Callum! Have I done something wrong?'

'I wouldn't know,' said Callum. He was a big handsome young Scotsman who had always been kind to Pippa. 'But I shouldn't think so. He seemed quite cheerful. Anghie's with him.' Anghie was Angharad. 'You'd better hurry.'

'Shouldn't I change first?'

'Of course not. Humphrey likes to see us hot from work.'

Pippa had only been in the Company since September, six months. Every autumn, at its headquarters in the midland city of Wolhampton, a few young men or girls were chosen from the ballet's upper school for the Company; only a few, two or three, sometimes none, this year only one, Philippa Fane – Pippa. 'I told you she was good,' the school's director had said to Cynthia, Pippa's mother.

Cynthia, though she, herself, was a teacher of mathematics, far removed from ballet, had done all she could to foster Pippa's dancing. It had been a hard struggle: Pippa's father, a young captain and Cynthia's only romance, had died soon after she was born, leaving them almost penniless and, 'I should never have succeeded,' Cynthia often said, 'if I hadn't come back to good old Wolhampton where, believe it or not, our big sprawling industrial city has its own ballet school and theatre, supported entirely by itself.' It also had its own sturdy young Company which, under the brilliant Humphrey Blair's direction, was coming to the forefront and attracting dancers of the standing of Jasper Christiansen, a young Dane, Isabelle Pascal from France and its own, home-trained principals like Faye Richardson and Maria Esslar who were making a name.

Cynthia knew only too well the demands that a professional talent makes: her husband's father had been an outstanding dancer with the Ballets Russes de Monte Carlo, later in Paris, though he was English. She knew, too, what it cost: extra lessons, which grew more and more expensive as the talent manifested itself, and shoes, shoes, shoes! It was an enormous relief when Pippa got into the junior ballet school on which Cynthia had set her sights, then into the upper school and, before her full time there was over, into the Company, 'Where she's *paid*,' said dazzled Cynthia.

Dazzled but not surprised. 'Talent often skips a generation,' she said. She knew Pippa had an affinity with the grandfather she had never seen – he had died too young. Pippa cherished his photographs, especially one as the Rose in *Spectre de la Rose* in which, after a ball, a young girl falls asleep and dreams that the rose she has been given that night changes into a virile young man who dances with her, until he ends with the leap out of the window that became famous in the ballet world. 'Monte Carlo, Vienna, Paris.' She would say those magical words over and over again.

Cynthia often worried over Pippa's dreaminess which was enhanced by the absolute obsession of most dancers with their dancing. 'They don't seem to think or talk about anything else, and can that be good for growing up?' The children did not even go to school and so meet ordinary people; the ballet school had its own academic staff where lessons had to be interwoven with the all-important dancing classes and rehearsals. 'So that they live in a world apart,' said Cynthia but had to add, 'Well, they have to.' All she could do was to be as practical – and sane – as possible.

Now Pippa picked herself up from the studio floor, put on her soft shoes, and pulled on the leg-warmers Cynthia had knitted for her – she was already in the warm sweater they all put on immediately after class. She still felt trickles of sweat running down from her hair – she had tied it up out of the way with a chiffon scarf – so she wiped her face and neck, gathered her paraphernalia into her bag and reluctantly went to Humphrey's office. With trepidation she knocked on the door.

'Come in.'

The only people in the office were the two most important in Pippa's dancing world: Humphrey Blair, artistic director and chief choreographer of the Midland Cities Ballet and Angharad Fullerton.

Humphrey, a gentle giant, seemed at first sight an unlikely person to be the director of an important ballet company; since he had almost retired as a dancer he had grown burly but could still be a towering Carabosse, the wicked fairy in *The Sleeping Beauty* or Doctor Drosselmeyer in *The Nutcracker*. Humphrey seldom lost his temper, yet he was firm and managed never to compromise; his blue eyes could change from lazy good humour to instant shrewdness and now they were appraising Pippa. 'Ah, Pippa!' he said. 'How are you? Enjoying life?'

'Yes, thank you,' but Pippa's lips were dry and her heart seemed to be beating in her throat.

'Pippa, you are a very lucky girl,' said Angharad, and she was smiling.

Pippa had come to idolize Angharad – Miss Fullerton to her – and was also a little afraid of her. To Pippa, Angharad's least word was law and she could be terrifying, withering in her sarcasm, but the dancers, as well as the hierarchy, knew that the Midland Cities Ballet would not have reached its high standard without her. 'She and Humphrey, and Pem, of course, make a good team,' said the principal dancers; Pem was Pax Pemberton, the ballet's musical director and conductor whom everyone called Pem.

Angharad, taller even than Juliet, the tallest of the girls in the *corps*, had, like Humphrey, put on weight since she stopped dancing and was now majestic. She had the whitest of skins, 'Impermeably white,' said Juliet who, to Pippa's astonishment, seemed to detest Angharad.

'How can you?' asked Pippa. 'I know she gets angry . . .'

'Angry Anghie,' sneered Juliet.

'But really she's kind.'

'To you, but she's a shit if she doesn't like you.'

'She seems to like us all.'

'It depends which way the wind blows.' Juliet, who had become Pippa's best friend, was not to be drawn.

Now Pippa felt only warmth and friendliness in the elegant woman sitting by Humphrey – Angharad was always well dressed. Her hair was still so flaxen it was almost white. 'She's pale all over. Ugh!' said Juliet. 'She's like one of those Medici statues in Florence, voluptuous but made of marble.' Angharad wore her hair in old-fashioned plaits round her head; when she was teaching it sometimes hung in a plait down her back. 'She's too old to wear it like that,' said the girls. 'She must be forty.'

'Poor old Angharad,' Humphrey often said. 'I don't envy her teaching girls,' but Pippa had always looked at Angharad's eyes, which were golden brown, sometimes soft with an unaccountable sadness that touched and puzzled Pippa who knew only too well how they saw everything and could harden into quick judgement. They were smiling now and she could not contain herself any longer.

'Why am I lucky? What did you want me for?'

'To go with the Company to Italy,' said Humphrey.

The Midland Cities Ballet was to make its North Italian tour in May and June, first to Venice, a short stay of a fortnight with only thirteen performances, then on to Verona, and for another two weeks in Milan. 'All important for us,' said Humphrey, 'the beginning, I hope, of our being better known abroad.'

It was a real exodus: he, his secretary and the Company manager were to go ahead to Venice with Robert Roberts the stage manager and his assistant – they would use each theatre's own Italian stage hands. The chief lighting designer went as well to set the lighting plan and make sure all the lights needed were in the theatre, or if not to hire them; again he would use each theatre's own staff.

Scenery, properties and wardrobe would go by van and be followed by the property master, wardrobe master and his assistant, the wardrobe mistress with hers, the wig master and his and the shoe lady for all the different shoes. There would be no dressers for the *corps* or soloists but the principals had the Company dresser.

The orchestra would travel by coach with a van for

their instruments. There would be a pianist for class and rehearsals – the piano in the pit had to be tuned afresh for each performance. Pax Pemberton preferred to travel on his own.

Angharad's assistant for the tour was the older Martha Trevelyan who had been in the Company for years and would take classes, and there were the dancers themselves: principals and soloists were booked by air, the *corps* by train. Angharad had chosen to travel with them: 'I can keep the excitement down,' and she warned the *corps*, 'You'll find it difficult to adjust. It won't be like dancing on your own stage.'

'Particularly the floors.' Constance had been on tour with other companies. 'There can be holes, even nails.'

'Robert will see to that,' said Angharad.

'I don't mind,' said insouciant Jenny. 'I'd dance on cobblestones to get to Venice.'

It had not been, at first, a unanimous choice to take Pippa. 'There are older, more experienced girls,' Humphrey told Angharad.

'That's precisely why. Pippa's so fresh – and isn't she one of our brightest hopes?'

'Which is why I feel she mustn't be forced in any way.'

'I'd see to that.'

'I'm sure you would, but Martha isn't certain that she's ready.' They all listened to Martha, yet though Pippa had only been in the Company for such a short while she had already been on tour with it – true, only in a minor way, and true, only locally, 'But you have seen how she took to it,' Angharad told Humphrey. 'She stood out and she *is* ready,' insisted Angharad.

'I don't understand you, Angharad. You're not usually so keen.'

'I understand myself only too well,' Angharad would have said had she been honest, and she seemed to see Pippa that morning as she had been in Angharad's bi-weekly class: 'lissome' was the word that came to Angharad for Pippa, lissome but strong; her skin had the cool smoothness of a petal. In Angharad's work she had, physically, to correct legs, arms, hands, necks and heads; it was a continual naked but legitimate touching – but Pippa's skin was so delicate that, 'Don't go into the hot sun,' Angharad wanted to tell her, knowing quite well Pippa would go into the sun. 'Well, the young throw away, with both hands, what they have.' Pippa's hair was brown – 'Mouse,' she would have said; Angharad knew how silky it was from when she had to alter the tilt of her head. Her eyes were deep blue and Angharad had seen how the long lashes curled against her cheek when Pippa, who had been so shy at first, looked at the floor every time Angharad came near her. 'And she works so hard and willingly in her efforts to please. If only she knew how she pleases me,' Angharad wanted to cry, but now in the office with Humphrey she managed to say, in her normal calm voice, 'Yes, I am keen. Call it instinct, Humphrey. I know, and you know, that for this Italian season we shall need everything we can get and Pippa is so appealing,' there was a slight tremor, 'yet sound in technique and you've already seen on stage how she stands out, or haven't you? Forgive me if I say that you often seem to take the *corps* for granted.'

'Only since you took it over.' Humphrey knew that his ballet mistress was on the verge of anger. 'I'm thinking of Pippa herself.'

'It will do her all the good in the world. She's such a naïve little thing, lived here in Wolhampton all her life and seldom been beyond it. She'll have to meet a totally different audience and for us it will be illuminating to see how she comes up to it, as I believe she will. Humphrey, she has to grow!'

'Very well. Call her in.'

Unaccountably Angharad wavered. 'If you really feel . . .'

He gave her his curiously sweet smile. 'Dear Angharad, if you hadn't convinced me, don't think for a moment I should let her come.'

'Why do you look so astonished?' he said now to Pippa in the office.

'I . . . I took it for granted I should stay behind.'

'We have asked your mother,' said Humphrey, 'and she is delighted.'

'You should have asked *me* and I would have told my mother.' There was a spark in Pippa that Humphrey, for one, was glad to see – 'She's not quite the naïve little sweet everyone seems to think' – but Angharad was not having any of that. 'We felt we had to ask your mother. Well, would you like to come?'

'I'm coming,' said Pippa.

'Cynthia,' Pippa always called her mother by her first name, 'Have we got a book about Venice?'

'I don't think so.' Then, 'Wait a minute,' said Cynthia, 'there was a book your grandfather had, old-fashioned and very sentimental but he loved it. It was about Venice.'

'What was it called?'

'*The City of Beautiful Nonsense.*'

'Beautiful nonsense! Lovely. Oh, Cynthia, find it. Please find it.'

At last Cynthia found it, a thick green book, its boards, lettered in gold, almost falling off, its paper thick. It was illustrated in black and white, rather dark full pictures and sketches of domed churches, canals, half-hooped bridges, houses with shutters, market stalls, squares, candles lit before altars, children playing, gondolas. As Pippa put it on the breakfast table it fell open at a page that had obviously been read over and over again: there, with a pencilled cross, was, 'You've got to see Venice'.

It was like a message from her grandfather and she read aloud:

'. . . you've got to see a city of slender towers and white domes, sleeping in the water like a mass of water lilies. You've got to see dark water-ways, mysterious threads of shadow, binding all these flowers of stone together. You've got to hear the silence in which the whispers of lovers of a thousand years ago, and the cries of men betrayed, all breathe and echo in every hush – these and the plash of the gondolier's oar or his call – "*Ohé!*" as he rounds a sudden corner. You've got to see it all in the night – at night, when the great white lily flowers are blackened in shadow, and the darkened water-ways are lost in an impenetrable depth of gloom. You've got to hear the stealthy creeping of a gondola and the lapping of the water against the slimy stones as it hurries by. In every light in barred windows up above, you must be able to see plotters at work, conspirators planning deeds of evil or a lover in his mistress's arms. You've got to see magic, mystery, tragedy, and romance, all compassed by stone and green water. A gondolier is not a London cabby. He plies that oar of his mechanically. He's probably dreaming too, miles away from us. There are some places in the world where it is natural for a man to love a woman, where it isn't a spectacle, as it is here, exciting sordid curiosity, and Venice is one of them.'

'Oh,' breathed Pippa and Cynthia did not laugh. 'It's a love story,' said Pippa with certainty and read on:

'And at night, when the whole city is full of darkness – strange, silent, mysterious darkness where every lighted taper that burns and every lamp that is lit seems to illuminate a deed of mystery – go out into the Grand Canal. It is so wonderful there. At last, one by one, the lights begin to go out. The windows that were alive and awake close their eyes and hide in the mysterious darkness; a huge white lamp of a moon glides up out of the breast of the Adriatic and then . . .'

'My dear child,' Cynthia was always sane, 'Venice may have been like that once but it's not now. It's decayed and smelly, crowded with tourists, noisy, especially the *vaporetti*, water-taxis, and motor barges. Not at all like that book now.'

'It's going to be,' vowed Pippa.

II

They came out of the train, which had been their home for nearly twenty-four hours by way of Paris and Milan, where Pippa had yearned to stop, on to the wide forecourt of Venice's station, which might have been any great station though better kept. For a moment they were stopped by the noisiness, the clamour of people – especially round the *vaporetto* quays – the bevy of motor-boats, but beyond was water, the water of the Grand Canal of this water-city flowing past. Though it looked slimy and full of debris its ripples glinted and they stood still to feel the balmy air and sun.

'Girls, come along, the *vaporetto* is just going,' Angharad called. She and some of the *corps* were already on board but Jenny had caught sight, on the opposite bank, of a fleet of gondolas moored, elbowed out by the water-taxis. 'Gondolas! Gondolas!' Her young voice rang out. There was an immediate answer from the opposite bank.

'*Si, si*, Signorina. Gondola. Gondola,' and several set out at full speed across the canal, their oars churning up the water in their haste. 'Gondola. Gondola.'

'*Girls!*'

Angharad's voice came from the ferry and the girls shouted back, 'We'll take the next ferry.'

'Gondola. Very cheap. *Very* cheap.'

They took three, piling in and, 'Pensione Benvenuto,' said Pearl.

The graceful elongated boats were all that Pippa had hoped, the prows ending in six silver prongs that showed

13

the six divisions of Venice; there were seats cushioned in black with fringes and down the length of the gunwales sea urchins made of brass held black cords for the nervous to hold on to if the water became rough. Their gondoliers stood on the planking of the stern with their great oars to guide and propel, one to each boat. They wore black jackets with collars like a sailor's, striped vests in red and white, narrow black trousers and, yes, gondolier straw hats with red ribbons round the crown, the ends hanging down. The gondolier of her boat had discarded his shoes.

'Ohé.' She had never felt anything like it, the forward glide, then a stroke of the oar from a strong arm sending them forward with a rippling sound, and an undulation side to side. She was sitting on the smaller cushioned seat, her back to the prow, and let her hand trail in the water.

'Better not,' said Constance. 'It's filthy.'

Pippa glanced quickly at their gondolier: had he heard that derogatory remark? If so he gave no sign. Probably doesn't speak English, thought Pippa, yet the gondoliers in the boats each side of them kept up a chatter in broken American and Italian to the other girls while he stayed silent. Then the gondolas left the press of traffic round the station, going under bridges from sunlight to shadow, into sunlight again, and came out to show the vista of the Grand Canal and here, indeed, were palaces, domes, towers.

It was a fleeting passage but they passed tall houses – which might have been palaces – in old stone, brick or stucco, coloured yellow, terracotta, grey, some balconied, some decorated with scrolled iron below their windows. Some had heavy studded front doors, steps going down into the water and gondola posts, striped red and white, like the gondoliers' vests, or blue and white. There were open squares and markets with, in the background, a church with a dome or campanile, houses huddled round them.

They passed a house hung with wisteria in blossom, caught a glimpse of lilac trees until spanning the width of the canal with a great single arch was a bridge of stone, weathered white, and Pippa felt impelled to ask the silent man, '*Per favore*, Rialto Bridge?' – she had been learning phrases from a paperback, *Italian in Three Months*.

'*Si*, Signorina.' Then he asked in English, 'The signorina knows our Rialto?'

'I . . . I have seen it in pictures.'

'Yes, it is the most famous bridge in the world.'

It was exactly like the illustration in her grandfather's green frayed book and, 'It's true! And it's still there!' She said it aloud and everyone laughed.

'Bridges don't run away,' said Pearl.

The gondolas turned one by one into a narrow canal, so narrow that the men sent whistles and cries of *ohé* warning ahead. There was barely room to pass other boats, barges, water-taxis that scraped house walls on either side or the stones of the also narrow, paved footpaths, the *fondamente*. They came to a small square that had a spreading tree and a little church with a low white dome, its pink walls banded with white marble. It had a curious appeal and Pippa asked, in English this time, 'What is that church?'

'The little church of San Giuseppe. You would say Saint Joseph,' he answered, in his polite English. 'It is dedicated to him and is much loved.'

'You speak very good English.'

'*Si*, Signorina.'

'But you are Venetian?'

'*Si*, Signorina.' No more than that and, as he rowed on, his eyes were dreamy. He's not aloof, thought Pippa. He's thinking of something else, and, He's different from the other men, she thought. To begin with he was younger – one of them was quite grizzled – not as thickset, smaller, slimmer, yet his gondola kept ahead of theirs.

Now he took off his hat, throwing it down by his bare feet: his hair was a mass of black curls – surely uncommon even in Italy? It fell to his neck and he had small gold rings in his ears; he wore a gold bangle – 'A bit of a dude.' Zoë, who was prim, disapproved, and Pippa found herself retorting, quite fiercely, 'He's not. He's just special.'

His face was piquant – she did not know how that word came to her – yet the brown eyes, that had been merry when he was touting for his gondola at the station, were elusive and, He could dance Puck in the *Dream*, she thought – dancing was never far away – but, 'Pippa, don't stare,' said Juliet, startling her and, as if to confound her, when one of the men shouted what she was sure was a ribald remark, his shout back seemed as bawdy as theirs.

He just doesn't choose to look at us, which nettled her. Well, he must take cargoes of tourists every day. I expect that's what we are to him, a cargo. Then, to confound her again, he began to sing. It was in English. '*West Side Story*, Maria's song "I'm pretty, I'm pretty",' whispered Jenny, only he sang, 'You're pretty,' smiling directly at Pippa with something so audacious, yet friendly in the way he said the words that she blushed scarlet.

As the song ended, the gondola came smoothly to a stop beside a flight of steps leading to a pair of high scrolled gates. Behind them, across a neat gravelled walk, was a big yellow house with green shutters; there was a glimpse of a garden, a shaven lawn as '*Siamo arrivati*,' he said. '*Ecco la Pensione Benvenuto.*'

'We won't do that again,' said Pearl when they had disembarked and she had paid him. 'It's exorbitant!'

'I'll do it whenever I can,' Pippa vowed silently. 'Even if it takes all my money,' and while the others, with their luggage, went through the gates, she lingered. The steps were guarded by a pair of small stone lions. She put her hand on their heads to feel their warm stone and carved manes. 'The signorina is paying her respects to the lions of Venice,' the gondolier said. He was standing in his boat. 'Good! Good!'

The *pensione* was a bad disappointment.

'It's English.'

'Imagine an English *pensione* in Venice.'

'How could they have done this to us?' cried the indignant girls. The principals were staying at the luxurious La Fenice et des Artistes near the opera house, soloists in a lesser hotel close by, the men of the *corps* in another, 'And I bet it's Italian,' grumbled the girls. 'Why this?'

'The Benvenuto has its advantages,' Angharad was to tell them when, coming to brief them, she heard their grievances. 'It's spotless and quite spacious, many *pensioni* are not, and you have that garden.' The garden, though, was as English as a Venetian garden could be, a lawn, herbaceous borders, clipped hedges, even a sundial. 'Above all,' said Angharad, 'it's healthy.'

'It's English.'

It was kept by a Major and Mrs Skinner – 'Skinner in Venice,' mourned Pippa. He, in his late fifties, was as English as his name, with his balding white hair – his scalp was pink – his white moustache and his pipe. He took *The Times*. She, a small plump lady, had freckled hands, blue eyes and carefully frizzed hair. They were excited and pleased to have the girls of the Company, 'We've never had dancers before,' and the welcome was enhanced by curiosity. 'We quite understand you have to work very hard and have unusual food times.'

'As if we were a strange species,' said Jenny.

'Well, we are,' said level-headed Constance.

Pippa thought the Skinners kind but even the food, to

17

which she had looked forward, was English. 'Roast beef, apple tart and custard for dinner.' Juliet read out the menu from its card by the lift.

'Yes, home from home,' said Mrs Skinner. 'We find our guests welcome it after too much Italian food.'

'But we haven't had any Italian food.'

After the joy of the gondola it was a sore disappointment but when they went up to their bedrooms to unpack and wash and Pippa saw the room she was to share with Juliet, she saw, too, that not all the Englishness of the Skinners had been able to transform the bedrooms of the old house: the floor was tessellated, the ceiling high – the two single white beds looked incongruous in it. The windows had heavy green shutters, closed now for the evening. Pippa opened them.

At once a hubbub of noise and life came in. She leaned out. This room was at the back of the *pensione*, overlooking crowded houses separated by alleyways; Mrs Skinner always apologized to guests for the noisiness of these back rooms – footsteps on flagstones, high jabbering voices, children screeching as they played and, floating over the housetops from some side canal, the noise of boat engines, a gondolier's whistle and '*Ohé.*' Pippa loved the noise. 'Those alleyways are the back kitchens of Venice,' Humphrey was to tell her.

'I love kitchens,' said Pippa.

She saw geraniums in window boxes, a bird in a cage hung in a window, washing drying, some on a line across the street, and on railings round curious little outbuildings like summerhouses on several rooftops. She saw a woman in one of them drying her long hair; it hung over the railing as she bent to call to somebody in the street below. A group of men were playing cards.

There was the sound of a clock striking and, as Juliet came to join her, bells began, bells near and far away, it seemed all over Venice. It was seven o'clock and, 'They are ringing the angelus,' said Juliet.

'The angelus?'

'In honour of the Virgin Mary. Listen.' Three peals, a pause, three peals, pause, two more peals then a small tumult of bells. I wonder if they are ringing in that little church of San Giuseppe? thought Pippa. I must find it.

Above the alleyways, houses and people she saw other buildings, campaniles, domes, turrets, not lily white, as in her grandfather's book; though some domes were white, most were all shades of brown, sepia, rose brown, pale brown that was almost cream, terracotta that was almost red. 'My grandfather said', Pippa told Juliet, 'that Venice is the most beautiful city on earth – *serenissima*, he called her.'

They had to go down. Angharad was coming.

'I have one thing to ask you,' Angharad ended by saying, 'a practical thing. You have had a long and tiring journey, I don't suppose many of you slept much last night and I want you at your best tomorrow. This Italian season is vital for us all – so please don't be tempted to go out tonight. Dinner has been ordered for you here – go to bed early and rest.'

She could not have spoken more tactfully, thought Pippa, but it was received in stubborn silence and, 'Who the hell does she think she is?' Zoë exploded when Angharad had gone.

'Nanny Angharad,' said Juliet.

'She was only thinking of us,' Pippa dared to say. She was still in awe of the other girls who seemed to her immensely worldly wise and sophisticated. 'Isn't she right to be concerned?'

'Not with our private affairs,' and Pearl said, 'Don't kid yourself. It's not us she's concerned with, it's our dancing.'

'Quite rightly.' Constance had to be fair.

'She's a fanatic. *I*, for one, am going out.'

'Me too.'

'And me.' It was a chorus.

Pippa was startled. She had taken it for granted that, though they might grumble, they would do as Angharad had asked and, 'But you can't. Angharad said . . .'

'We know what Angharad told us, thank you.'

'She didn't tell, she asked.'

They were amazed that this comparatively new girl, who had always seemed so shy, should contradict Pearl. It must be Venice, thought Juliet, remembering Pippa in the gondola that afternoon and how, suddenly, she had shone.

The young men and women in the *corps* had respect for Angharad, they all knew what they owed to her, but Pearl was losing patience. 'I think we know more about Angharad than you do, Miss Know All.'

That stung. What they did not know was how Pippa had had to nerve herself to defy Pearl because she passionately believed that if you revered – and perhaps loved – someone you had to defend them. 'She only asked.'

'Which doesn't mean we have to answer. Jenny, phone the boys' hotel. Constance, you're the tactful one, tell Mrs Skinner we're sorry but we'll be out for dinner. We'll all go together then we'll be doing', she mocked Pippa, 'what your precious Angharad said.'

'She's not my precious but she did ask.'

'You stay in, then.'

'But I don't want to, any more than you do.'

'Please yourself.' Pearl shrugged.

'I'm not pleasing myself,' said Pippa miserably.

'Then come, and don't make such a fuss,' whispered Juliet. 'Angharad's not all that important.'

'Very well, I'll come.'

'How kind of you,' gibed Jenny, and Pearl said, 'I don't think we want you,' and she too gibed, 'Anghie's pet should have an early night and go to bed.'

'Little Saint Pippa,' said Constance.

III

Pippa lay on her bed where she had thrown herself in the empty room. She was too shocked and bewildered to cry. *I only tried to be fair, then why? Why?* They must hate me, thought Pippa. She was also hungry but Constance had cancelled their dinner and, *I don't want to ask Mrs Skinner. Could I go out by myself?* But after what Angharad had said, she did not dare. The long empty evening stretched ahead.

She might really have cried when there was a knock at the door. Sniffing back tears she had to open it. 'Telephone, Signorina.' It was the hall porter, Beppo. 'All other misses gone out.'

It was Angharad. 'Who is that?'

'Pippa.'

'I asked for Pearl. I want to speak to her about tomorrow.'

'Pearl's out.'

'Out! When I specially . . . Constance, then.'

'She's out, too. They all are.'

'Except you?'

'Yes.' A small sob escaped.

'Why, Pippa?'

'You – you asked us not to go out.'

There was a moment's silence. Then, 'You mean you stayed in because I . . .'

'I suppose so.'

Another silence. *Is she going to be cross too? I never do anything right,* thought Pippa.

Then Angharad asked, 'Have you had dinner?'

'There isn't any dinner. They – we – cancelled it.'

She might excusably be cross but the voice Pippa knew so well said, 'Listen, Pippa. You're coming out to have dinner with Humphrey, Pem and me.'

'Mr Blair! Pem! You!' Pippa could not believe her ears.

'Yes. I have to go out. The cook in this flat I've been lent is off on Sunday. They're coming with me. Pem knows a good fish restaurant quite near you. Don't put on anything grand – it's quite ordinary – but a dress would be nice.' And Angharad said, her voice soft, 'Isn't it a bit forlorn alone in that *pensione* your first night in Venice?'

'It is. It *is!*'

'We'll call for you in ten minutes. Go and change.'

In the balmy noisy Venetian night with myriads of lights, illuminated domes and bridges, Pippa slipped through the *pensione* gates to wait by the stone lions where she could see the traffic of boats on the Grand Canal. As she stood there, she heard music, and a flotilla of gondolas passed slowly, the black hulls so close they seemed tied together and, in one, a singer stood under a light singing to an accordion player – the music seemed to come to Pippa's feet. Above all the lights, she could see stars, faintly spangled, a half-moon; her heart seemed to fly up to them as a water-taxi came to the steps, Angharad stepped out, put an arm round her shoulders in a quick hug and, 'Poor little Cinderella,' said Humphrey.

'How sweet you look,' said Pem. 'We can walk from here,' he told them. 'But be careful how you step.'

They went through alleyways to a broader street edged with shops, leading from a bridge into a surge of people, still buying and selling, vegetables, fruit, cheeses. There was a bakery with newly baked bread and a delicious smell – At this hour! thought Pippa. A pâtisserie had delectable-looking cakes and tarts – she had not known quite how hungry she was. A pierrot doll turned in the window of a gift shop. There were jewellers' shining with gold. 'They're all still open,' she marvelled.

'Well, in Italy they close from about noon till four o'clock for lunch and the siesta when everyone sleeps . . .'

'Everyone?'

'Not the tourists, who are bewildered, poor souls, and wander about wondering what has happened,' said Pem, 'but most Italians sleep, even the donkeys, goats and cats, even the winged lion on the pillar at San Marco.'

'You're teasing.'

Pippa walked with Pem, Humphrey and Angharad ahead, she in a white dress, a shawl-scarf in vivid red round her shoulders. She looks lovely, thought Pippa as the blonde hair shone in the lights. She, herself, was at ease with Pem; he gave her singing lessons as he did to a few of the Company, but to her he had said seriously, 'You know, Pippa, you could have another career in *lieder* – songs, not opera. You'll never have the power for that, but you could do well with *lieder* if you worked.'

'How could I work at that and dancing?'

'There we go,' said Pem.

Now he held her arm, guiding her through the crowd past lit stalls, some with coloured lights. Pippa seemed to be walking on air; only Pem's hand held her down. Then they came to a wide-open door, with over it a fish turning like the pierrot doll in the gift shop window, a fish with scaled metallic sides. 'Il Pescatore Carlo' said a notice.

Pem led the way and at once, 'Signor! Signor Pemberton!' A rotund little man with a high colour and big moustaches was pumping Pem's hand, his brown eyes delighted. '*Benvenuto*. Welcome, *è un piacere rivederla*. Good to see you again, Signor,' he said to Humphrey, '*Signora graziosa*,' to Angharad and, when Pem introduced

Pippa, '*Graziosa, che bella!*' said Carlo. '*Non ci sono ragazze come voi Inglesi!*'

'He says there are no young girls like the English,' Pem told Pippa.

'*Si! Bellissima!*'

'Pippa, this is Carlo. He has the best and most famous fish restaurant in Venice – or, shall we say, all Italy,' and reserved Pem slapped Carlo on the back.

When Carlo laughed his moustaches shook, his rubicund face crinkled until his eyes disappeared. 'We are lucky too,' Pem went on. 'Usually Carlo throws Americans and the English out, "Sorry, no tables", when the tables are obviously empty.'

'Not true! I have many good English and American clients, but your little friend is charming. This way.' He led them to a corner table. At once two bottles of wine appeared.

They were, for Venice, early and most of the restaurant was empty. At first sight it looked plain, a big room of small tables and one long one, made of tables set together, whitewashed walls, a wooden floor. Pippa would have expected a fish restaurant to have seashore paintings, stuffed fish, nets, shells, but the walls were simply whitewashed and, as they took their places, she saw that the red and white checked cloths were linen, the napkins starched; on every table was a single red carnation in a silver vase, the table silver shone and when Carlo poured the wine the glasses were of fine thin glass. No candles. 'People must see what they eat,' Carlo always said. The wine was 'with the compliments of the house'. A waiter brought a platter of canapés, minuscule biscuits spread with pâté, tiny puffs of pastry with shrimp and two-inch squares of bread with what looked to Pippa like glistening black granules. 'What is it?'

'Caviare.'

'Do we *eat* it?'

'Indeed we do.' They all laughed.

'Well, let's order,' said Pem. 'It takes quite a time because everything is cooked fresh.'

Carlo himself brought the menus. 'Tonight we have . . . *seppie in umido.*'

'What's that?' asked Pippa.

'Squid cooked in its own ink. I should choose something else.' Pem had seen her small shudder.

The menu was long, hand-written in Italian; she looked at it helplessly. It was Humphrey who came to her rescue.

'What about starting with one of those little melons that are so good just now? Then a fish soup . . .'

'*Fish* soup?'

'They are noted for it here. Then, as it's your first visit to Italy, why not have pasta? Try this. Cannelloni *alla* Carlo.'

It was a dinner such as Pippa had never imagined. The melon came, a whole small melon in a silver cup filled with crushed ice. 'Heavenly!' she said as she took the first spoonful. The fish soup, though she tasted it cautiously, was delicious. On her cannelloni a waiter sprinkled grated Parmesan and pepper from a giant pepper pot. Angharad had an escallop of veal, sliced thin with herbs and butter, Humphrey, '*granseola all'olio e limone,*' he told her – crab with oil and lemon – while Pem, to her amazement, had a dish of paper thin sliced beef with grated Parmesan. 'Is it *raw*?' asked Pippa.

'It is,' said Pem, and ate happily.

Best of all was the dessert, which Humphrey chose for her. 'You must have some tiramisu.'

'And how do you make this delectable concoction?' Angharad asked Carlo.

'That is Carlo's secret.' His moustaches quivered with pleasure. 'But for you, Signora, I will tell you, but perhaps not all. First you make a cake. What you call a sponge, I think. It must be light, light as air.' His hands showed how light. 'Then slice it, dip it in strong, strong black coffee. Then put in a bowl alternating each slice with rich Italian cream cheese whipped together with egg yolks and sugar. The last layer is sprinkled with chocolate powder, thick, it must cover the cheese. Let it stand, then say a little prayer as you serve it.'

'Once you eat that, Pippa,' said Humphrey, 'you won't be able to dance any more.'

Before Pippa could do more than taste it, there was a burst of loud noise, men's and women's voices vociferous and a stampede of feet as if the street were coming in. Carlo darted to Pem's side. 'It is the party. The Mayor of Patavia and his friends, dignitaries and their wives, very high people. They cannot relax in their own town, they have to keep their positions, so they come to Venice. I hope they are not too noisy.'

They were noisy. All conversation was drowned in the drinking, toasting, complimenting Carlo, the men's voices the loudest, the women shrill. 'They are all old.' Pippa was disappointed. 'I suppose mayors have to be old.'

'Middle-aged,' said Angharad.

'But young tonight.' Carlo was benign. The Mayor was a favourite patron.

There were only three ladies, all plump, dark hair and eyes, well dressed. 'Italian women dress beautifully,' Angharad told Pippa. 'Look at those black velvet trousers and that tunic, so expensively simple, so chic, the great gold earrings, and gold shoulder bag – that must be Gucci.'

The men were in suits that looked too thick for the night and made Humphrey's white polo-necked silk jersey and blue slacks, Pem's pale grey jacket and trousers more than elegant.

The party grew more noisy but it was a noise of

warmth and bonhomie. 'All the same,' Pem was saying, 'I think we'll go and have our coffee in that little café over the bridge,' when the Mayor, obviously the Mayor, his face rosy, his coat open to show a well-fed stomach, stood up and called across the restaurant to them. 'He hopes', Pem translated, 'they are not too noisy but it's his birthday.'

At the same time a waiter brought a tray with four glasses of brandy: '*Coi complimenti del sindaco* – from the Mayor.'

'Brandy! That's uncommon,' said Pem. 'It's usually grappa or whisky. I suppose it's because we're English. A real compliment.'

But Pippa said, 'Such big glasses for such a little drink.'

'We must drink his health,' said Humphrey.

They stood up, glasses in hand. '*Salute!*'

Angharad began, 'Happy birthday to you . . .' They all joined in. 'Happy birthday, Signor Mayor.'

'*Buon compleanno!*' called Pem. There was clapping and laughing and, as if it had chosen that moment, from outside came music, the sound of a guitar and an accordion, which had taken up the birthday tune. Led by Pem it was sung again, then they sat down to wild applause, but the music went on. Pippa, back into her tiramisu, had not seen that the musicians had come into the restaurant and were serenading the ladies in Italian.

They had their backs to her but there was no mistaking that head of curls and, 'It's my gondolier,' she almost said it aloud. His voice, as she knew already, was full, sweet-toned. He played the guitar, his companion, young too, playing an accordion, looked stocky beside him. They were not dressed in their striped vests but wore crimson shirts and sashes; their shoes were so polished they flashed. Obviously known to Carlo, they went to each lady in turn, making them laugh and bridle, playing their instruments near but softly tantalizing, her gondolier singing.

'I wish they would come to us,' said Pippa.

As if in answer they came. He obviously recognized Pippa and smiled, but diplomatically went first to Angharad looking with admiring eyes at her blonde hair and fairness. *'La bella signora!'* they sang.

'They think you're married to Humphrey,' Pem teased Angharad. Then they turned to Pippa and sang so seductively that, as before, she blushed.

At each song the Mayor's party clapped – a waiter brought wine for the young men, sent by the Mayor. Then Pem said, 'Pippa, let's give them a song. What about the drinking song from *Traviata*? They can be the chorus. I'm sure they'll know it.'

He and she had sung it together many times. For a moment she was taken aback, then nodded as Pem began the rollicking tune – he had a fine tenor voice. *'Liba mo, liba mo me lie-ti culici.* Let's drink.' Pippa took up Violetta's part, the guitar and accordion joining in; when it came to the chorus everyone sang, even the waiters; it ended in a tumult of laughter and clapping.

As they sank back in their chairs, 'Now, Pippa,' said Pem, 'you sing alone.'

Angharad thought she would refuse but Pippa stood up and tossed off the brandy – 'In one go,' Angharad remonstrated. 'You're meant to sniff and sip it.'

Pippa did not hear, she beckoned to the guitarist. 'You know "Santa Lucia"?'

For answer he played the opening bars.

Silence fell as Pippa sang. If Pem's voice was fine, Pippa's was like a flute, fresh, clear. She was wearing a sleeveless dress that Cynthia had made for her, strawberry pink with white piping that showed off her neck and arms, glowing with young firm smoothness. Her hair had been brushed to silk – all the dancers tended their hair; in her excitement her eyes looked amazingly blue. 'She's a pretty thing,' Pem whispered to Angharad who could not take her eyes off Pippa and, 'I was right,' she whispered back, 'there is a spell.'

Even the waiters hushed, standing still, and when the song ended there was a sigh that ran round the room until the applause broke with cries of '*Brava! Brava! Bis!*'

'Signorina . . .'

The clapping went on.

'Signorina.' It was her guitarist gondolier. 'I think you should sing "I'm pretty".' He began to play it and her voice seemed to soar effortlessly in the room.

It ended, she sat down, her face flushed – the brandy had begun to work – and the Mayor came up and kissed her hand.

'Gondola. Gondola.'

They had walked back towards the *pensione* and when they came to the narrow canal a gondola was waiting. Angharad paused. 'Perhaps we should take the gondola home. Our friends from Patavia may be on the *vaporetto* and it might be a bit much.'

'Yes, I'll just see Pippa in,' but Angharad had seen her face as she realized she was not to go in the gondola.

'The evening's over,' she could not help saying in desolation.

'It's nearly midnight. Don't you want it to be over?'

'Not yet.'

She was still lit with the warmth of success, and felt as if she were walking on air. 'That's the wine and the brandy. You're not accustomed to it,' Angharad could have said, but she relented. 'Suppose we go for a little trip first. Our heads need clearing – I know mine does. We'll take Pippa then drop her back.'

'*Please.*' Pippa said it so fervently that they all laughed. 'A gondola ride would be perfect. Perfect!'

As she stepped down into the gondola she saw it was her musician gondolier again. She smiled at him; he clapped his hand to his heart, pressing it, and she laughed aloud.

She had dutifully sat down on the smaller seat that faced him but Angharad beckoned her to the cushions of the bigger one and Pippa moved over beside her.

It was, as she had said, the perfect end to a perfect evening and as unexpected as it was perfect. The gondola turned into the Grand Canal past the houses and palaces, the windows of some still lit, others dim, past a floodlit church, a flight of steps with a single lamp-post, the lights of a crowded *vaporetto*. There were still many boats, some with lanterns – the lantern of their own gondola sent a small path of light as it was reflected in the water.

The gondolier began to sing. Pem laughed and said, 'There, Pippa, that's for you.'

'What is he singing?'

'A Venetian song. "Un' Inglesina sul Canal Grande". "An English girl on the Grand Canal".'

When the song ended she turned to the gondolier, '*Grazie*. Thank you.'

'*Grazie mille*, Signorina.'

Soon the gliding rhythm of the gondola, the gentle push of the oar, the slight rolling were lulling. Pippa's eyes felt heavy, sleep was overcoming her and without knowing it, her head dropped to Angharad's shoulder.

Angharad put an arm round her, drawing her closer. Only the gondolier saw her kiss Pippa's hair.

The bump of the gondola against the steps of the *pensione* woke Pippa. 'I must have been asleep.'

'You were,' and, 'So much for the gondola ride!' the men teased her.

She stumbled up the steps. 'I had better walk you in,' said Pem.

It was when, having taken Angharad to her flat, he was paying off the gondola at his and Humphrey's hotel that the gondolier said, '*Per favore*, Signor, what is the name of the little signorina?'

Pem gave him a hard look. 'That, I think, is none of your business.'

The young man did not scowl. On the contrary he smiled sweetly as if Pem were of no consequence and said, in an English that surprised Pem, 'Simple. Carlo will tell me.'

IV

'Where did you go?'

Pippa had come in so softly that Juliet had not woken; she had simply slipped off her dress and gone straight to bed. She could have slept through the morning but, 'Pippa, wake up.' Juliet shook her. 'Where were you? I took ages to get to sleep I was so worried,' and, as Pippa sat up, 'Whew! You stink!'

'I expect it was the brandy.'

'Brandy? Beppo said you had gone out with a lady and two gentlemen.'

'So I did.'

'Who were they?'

Pippa had to hedge. 'If I were you,' Pem had said at the door of the *pensione*, 'I shouldn't tell the others where you've been tonight,' and now, 'People,' said Pippa.

'You don't know any people in Venice.'

'Don't I?'

'No, you don't,' and, 'They came by water-taxi. Pippa, it was Angharad, wasn't it?'

'Yes.'

'After she told us not to go out!'

'She had to go. She has been lent a flat and the cook has Sundays off. Yes, Angharad, Humphrey and Pem,' it was a happy chant, but to her surprise Juliet came close, a serious Juliet.

'Pippa, don't let yourself be duped by Angharad.'

'Duped. What a horridly unpleasant word, when she's so kind to me.'

'Wake up.' Juliet was still intensely serious. 'Listen, I know. I ought to know.'

'Know what? If it's something against Angharad I don't want to hear. I won't listen. Why shouldn't she be kind to me? And if she is, why shouldn't I be grateful? I am grateful. Why not?'

Juliet was patient enough to make one more effort. 'Pippa, think. People seldom do anything without a reason.'

'What reason could she possibly have except my dancing? I know she cares about that, but then she cares for all of us. Perhaps it's because I'm good – I can't help knowing I'm good – I think you're just plain jealous.'

'Thank *you*.' Juliet turned her back.

'I think you're all very unfair to Angharad. She gave me a marvellous time and I think she's utterly marvellous, so there.'

As Angharad had told them, they walked easily to La Fenice. 'Once upon a time anyone who was anyone used the water entrance but now it's too expensive, the *vaporetto* can't get down the narrow canal.' Juliet had read her guide book. Crossing the Grand Canal they found their way through alleys and streets, sometimes using the *fondamente*.

All at once Pippa paused. On a wall beside one of the innumerable small bridges on their way was a niche with a painting of the Madonna behind a gold mesh; there were fresh flowers in the vases below her. She was evidently a beneficent madonna: her smile seemed to go far down the narrow canal. She's smiling as if she's welcoming me, thought Pippa. She stood still to look until Juliet jerked her. 'Come *on*.'

Pippa still gazed. 'You wouldn't see that in Wolhampton.'

'You wouldn't expect to,' said Juliet.

The outside of La Fenice was dull – it might have been a theatre anywhere – but going round to the stage door they saw a small courtyard apart, its walls on three sides creeper-hung, a great stone urn in its centre, the canal running beside it. It looked private. Was it where the Venetian socialites came out, Pippa wondered, to catch a breath of air and smell the roses? Or an actor, perhaps, or maybe two for an assignation during their performance? Music would have spilled over into this little space and, in those days, there would have been no fumes or stale smell from the canal, only ripples . . . She stood, fascinated, until Juliet took her by the elbow.

Robert Roberts showed them over the theatre. The auditorium was delightful. 'Well, it's supposed to be the prettiest theatre in Europe,' he told them. The seats were rose velvet edged with gilt, its ceiling and proscenium painted with angels in a blue sky and heavily scrolled. The first three tiers were all boxes. 'Once upon a time,' Robert told them, 'the Venetian grandees all had a box because it was the cheapest way of seeing their friends and acquaintances. Hardly anyone looked at or listened to the play or opera, they were too busy gossiping.'

'Thank goodness they don't do it now,' said Pearl.

There was a good rehearsal room, a large studio with *barres*, one large dressing room for the girls of the *corps*, another for the young men. 'But there aren't nearly enough mirrors,' complained Robert. 'We need thirty-five for making up alone.'

Everyone's chief anxiety, though, was for the stage floor: its wood was in a reasonable state but it was in sections, the joins made smooth by wide Scotch tape, which seemed amateurish, and, 'We won't like that,' said Pearl.

'You won't have to,' said Robert. The Company's own heavy vinyl floor cloth had travelled with them; Robert and the stage hands would make sure it was flat, firm, and would not move.

'Or else, God help us,' said Constance.

'It won't move,' he promised.

'At least there's space,' said Pearl. 'On tour in England we sometimes have to dance in one another's elbows.'

Soloists' and principals' rooms were above, and above them were the wardrobe rooms. Bertha Maguire, the wardrobe mistress, was loud in complaints about the dust. 'You'd think these rooms hadn't been used for years.' Particularly at risk were the gauzy tarlatan skirts of the white costumes for *La Bayadère*. They seemed to pick up the dust. The wardrobe master complained the same, while the wig master was in despair. 'All those white wigs for *The Tales of Hoffman*!' The shoe lady had a cupboard of a room – Robert had had to put up pigeon holes for her: 'I don't think they've had ballet here for a long time' – and behind everything was a clatter of feet on the back staircase which, being iron-bound with scrolled iron banisters, was incredibly noisy – during a performance anyone using them had to walk on tiptoe.

For this Italian tour, the Midland Cities Ballet had two programmes to be given alternately: one was a double programme, the first act of *La Bayadère* and the chess ballet *Checkmate*, which had been so successful and exciting in 1937 and which Humphrey had revived, keeping it exactly as it was when Dame Ninette de Valois originally produced it, her third major ballet. The Red Knight would be danced by Jasper Christiansen, the Black Queen by Maria Esslar. Pippa, partly because she was small, was a red pawn.

She was in *La Bayadère* too. Angharad had been instrumental in the choice of this ballet because no other better showed the quality of her beloved *corps* than its first act: the girls, in classical white gauzy long dresses, all twenty of them with a few soloists, had to come, one by one, to the top of a ramp and hold an *arabesque* for some moments before going down to her place on stage in what had to be an exact alignment of dancers, whose heads and eyes moved as one. They were led by Pearl. Juliet as the tallest was last. 'The *corps de ballet* moved with silent smooth precision and musicality', one critic had written of the Midland Cities Ballet. That made Angharad proud.

'It's a good life in the *corps*,' she often said. 'You are doing what you want to do, are well paid and there's less of the strain, the torments and the nerves that principals, even stars, go through, and don't forget, for every princi- pal dancer we need at least six in the *corps*. They truly are the body of the Company.'

To Humphrey though, the more important pro- gramme was his new version of *The Tales of Hoffman*. Jasper, again, would dance the profligate poet, Hoffman; for the next major male role of Niklaus, Hoffman's friend, guide and protector, Humphrey had chosen a gifted dancer, Maurice Le Roy whose slight femininity fitted the role – in the ballet's epilogue he would be transformed into the Spirit of Poetry.

There were three equal female parts, each figuring as Hoffman's love in each of the three acts: Olympia, the mechanical doll of act one, was Faye Richardson, Jasper's normal partner; Giulietta, the brazen courtesan of act two,

was Maria; while Antonia, a young, innocent girl in act
three, was danced by Isabelle Pascal, who was rapidly
making her mark.

Pippa was one of the gypsies who came to entertain
the guests at the ball given for Olympia and, more
importantly, one of eight girls chosen to dance the barcarolle in act two, Offenbach's famous Barcarolle – the
melody came from a Venetian boat song, which made the
ballet peculiarly suited to Venice.

The Company went straight into routine. 'We haven't
even looked at Venice yet,' some grumbled, knowing
very well they were there to dance, not to look.

It was strenuous but they were used to that; first the
necessary Company class taken by Martha, then rehearsal
with Angharad and, often, Humphrey, which might keep
them until two, even three; then there might be stage calls
and, until the première, another class at five thirty. There
were also tasks: visits to Wardrobe for repairs, to the shoe
lady for another pair of *pointe* shoes that had to be broken
in. Hair had to be washed. 'And we are supposed to rest.'
It was beginning to be hot. When the performances started
it would be worse. The six o'clock Company class would
then become a 'warming up' session, though as soon as a
dancer felt warmed and relaxed, he or she could leave, but
it would not be worthwhile going back to *pensioni* or
hotels, as all of them had to make up, dress, and be ready,
calm and quiet, to answer their initial stage call. 'Then
you'll come under the spell of the overture, which takes
you right into the ballet,' said Angharad, 'and you cease
to be Faye or Maria or Isabelle – or any of yourselves,
even Pippa – for the magical space of the evening when
you are Olympia, Giulietta, Antonia, and make the audience believe in them. Ballet truly can cast a spell,' said

Angharad. 'I shall never forget the first time I saw *Petrushka* – I broke my heart.'

After a performance it usually takes dancers some time to unwind and they are always hungry.

The principals ate in the exclusive – and expensive – Bar Al Teatro in the square outside the theatre; floodlit at night, it looked itself like a stage set. For the others, meals were available at some of their hotels, the Pensione Benvenuto had agreed to serve a late supper, but Callum, who made himself at home anywhere, had discovered the Trattoria da Nino, one of the small cafés well away from the Grand Canal and the piazza San Marco where everything was expensive. 'This is real Venice,' said Callum.

'It's certainly smelly,' said Pearl. The stench of the canal mingled with the smell of cooking, particularly of fish and garlic, of coffee from the machines, wine spills, warm bread and the pungent scent of the pink geraniums in boxes along the railings, but the dancers soon adopted it as their own, calling the proprietor Nino as if they had known him all their working lives and, after they had eaten simple dishes, pasta or sandwiches Italian style – half a crusty stick loaf with smoked ham or salami – they stayed late drinking, a cheap white wine Callum had learned of from the gondoliers, or Campari, fresh orange juice or cappuccino.

When Juliet and Pippa walked back to the *pensione* and passed the Madonna, Pippa saw she was lit by votive lamps. It made a small warm remembrance to take back to bed. 'But I wish I could stay up all night,' said Pippa.

'Think how you would dance next day if you did,' said Juliet, and, even in her Venice transport, Pippa could see the sense of that.

She had made it up with Juliet. 'I'm sorry I said you were jealous. It was silly of me.'

'Yes, it was,' said Juliet, who was big enough to bear no rancour, though tacitly neither of them mentioned Angharad again. More and more Pippa appreciated the sense and kindness of her handsome dark and showy friend. Juliet was showy.

'Everything that girl dances she makes common,' Pem had said.

'Which can be valuable,' said Humphrey. 'For instance, I'm not sure she doesn't make a better Giulietta courtesan than Maria,' whom Juliet was understudying.

That second night they had supper in the *pensione*, though Pippa chafed.

'We have to think of money,' said Juliet. 'We're spending far too much.'

'I don't care,' said Pippa. 'I want to be out.'

'Venice seems to have gone to your head.'

'Yes, I want it to.'

'Your grandfather always said', Cynthia had told Pippa, 'that if you want to know a town, go to its cemetery and its markets.'

' "Venice's cemetery, centuries old, is on the island of San Michele, where they say" ', Juliet read from her guide book, ' "the soil is all bones." '

Pippa shuddered. 'In my grandfather's book there's a wonderful open-air market near the Rialto. Let's get up early and see if we can find it.'

'We'd be late for class.'

'Not if we went very early and took the *vaporetto*.'

'It's risky.'

'Juliet, we must see *something*.'

'Well we mustn't linger.'

They lingered.

The market was as enchanting as it was business-like. The sun filtered through its awnings, making alleyways of light between the stalls set out with vegetables. 'Not just heaped up as they do in England,' said Pippa, but arranged with designer care: mounds of clean pale new potatoes, green vegetables fresh as spring, carrots washed and tied together in carrot bouquets, bundles of asparagus built into pyramids, their heads exactly matched, the brilliant red of tomatoes, small globes of mushrooms, still with dew on them, pans of water in which trimmed hearts of artichoke floated and, on a special tray, infant artichokes still in foliage, prominently displaying their price.

'A thousand lire.'

'Do they mean a dozen?'

'A thousand *each*!' Juliet had a smattering of Italian.

There was every kind of fruit. They had a glass of fresh-squeezed orange juice. 'But it's red.'

'Blood oranges,' said experienced Juliet. They ate apples warm with the sun.

Then, somewhere near, above their heads, bells began to ring for Mass. 'God! It's twenty to ten,' cried Juliet. 'Come on.'

'We'll miss half.' Pippa was rebellious. 'Let's miss it altogether.'

'Don't be an idiot, Angharad will skin us. Come on.'

'So!' said Angharad to Pippa. 'Martha tells me you had only twenty minutes of class.'

'We ran. Truly we did.'

'I thought you took your dancing seriously.' Pippa could see that Angharad was angry, 'Angry Anghie' as the dancers called her, but now she was unreasonably angry; there was hardly a dancer who at one time or another had not been late for class, but up to now neither Pippa nor Juliet had been a minute late.

'I knew it was wrong,' Pippa pleaded, 'but we thought

41

we had plenty of time and it was so fascinating.' She was still lit by the sheer joy of the market.

'Do you think we brought you to Venice to be fascinated?' Then Angharad softened. 'It's not like you, Pippa. You mustn't let Juliet lead you on.'

'It was I who led her. It was my idea,' but Angharad was going on: 'You may not understand, Pippa, but Juliet always takes a peculiar pleasure in undermining me, and she knows what I am trying to build on your dancing. Haven't I always guarded you?'

'Yes. Yes.' Pippa was becoming distressed. 'I can never be grateful enough.'

'Then don't hobnob with Juliet.'

'But she's my best friend.'

'If you would rather that than being, as you used to be, loyal to me.'

'Why can't I be loyal to both?' Pippa could see no reason.

Led by Juliet and Callum, the others were kinder to Pippa now, not only Pearl and Constance but Jenny, Anne Marie, Gilda, Zoë and the rest of the girls, Dermot, Henry, Pat and Ray among the men, all of them as eager, as excited by the Italian season as she, which should have made her in tune with them but, Don't dancers ever talk about anything but dancing? she wondered, and on Tuesday afternoon, 'I'm going to the big café on the piazza,' she announced.

'Florian's, and pay four times as much for a cappuccino,' said Callum, but Pippa felt she had plenty of money. 'After all, we're paid extra every day we're abroad.'

She did not want to spend it on souvenirs, though she meant to buy a pair of gloves for Cynthia. 'They have the most exquisite gloves in Venice,' Constance had told her.

'And bags and shoes,' but, 'I'd rather spend on places like Florian's or Carlo's' – though she did not think she would have the chance to go to Carlo's again – 'or going in a gondola,' she told Pearl.

'But St Mark's piazza is where the tourists flock.'

'I wouldn't mind being a tourist, then I could spend the whole day looking.'

The strange part was that she, who had been so gratified in being one of the Company, so hurt when the girls shut her out and happy to be taken back again, now wanted to look by herself, simply sitting in the sun, not talking but watching the people and the pigeons under a sky so blue it might have been painted above the pageant of the piazza, its colonnades, the domes – Always domes, thought Pippa – and carved front of the Basilica, its campanile – Always campaniles – the clock, the rosy façade of the Doge's palace. It did not occur to her to go inside any of them, she only wanted to watch, even the tourists and the pedlars, stalls selling gimcrackery, toys, garish pictures of Venice framed in startling gilt, coins, beads, chiffon scarves, cheap gondolier hats.

The hats brought her gaze to the waterfront beyond the winged lion on his pedestal – he reminded her of the lions at the *pensione*; she had come to call them her lions. The water round the piazza was rough from the press of traffic, *vaporetti* coming and going, barges, cargo-boats, water-taxis sending up a wash. Behind them, across the water, was the great white church of the Salute but Pippa was at present hardly interested in churches – Except I should like to see that little church of San Giuseppe again.

The gondolas were moored along the wide waterfront of the Riva degli Schiavoni beside the piazza. Pippa had looked there and in the shelters where the boatmen rested for her musician gondolier but could not see him. Well, he must have hundreds of passengers, she told herself, of course, he has forgotten.

V

'*Una delle subrettine a casa mia* – a showgirl in my home. *Mai! Mai!* Never.' For the third time Nicolò was badgering his mother and for the third time Leda was refusing.

'Mamma, I've told you. She's not that kind of dancer. She's with a ballet company. I've told you, they are opening at La Fenice on Wednesday. She's an artist, Mamma.'

'Hmph!' was all Leda would say.

Leda ruled absolutely in the small flat up three flights of steep stairs, 'So steep and the flat so small,' Nicolò continually complained.

'Well, your father was brought up here and with seven other children.'

'Where did they sleep?'

'With each other, and did what their parents told them.'

Nicolò had been fourteen when his father died but Leda had not let him go out to work as Nicolò would dearly have liked to. 'He must finish school,' she had said, and went out to work herself. She was fiercely protective of Nicolò; his father had never amounted to anything and all Leda's ambitions were set on her son, but lately Nicolò had eluded her, charmingly, of course – Nicolò was never rude or cavalier. She had planned that he would go to college, even university, and perhaps find work in a government office with chances of promotion – and here he was, a gondolier.

The disappointment had been mitigated when, through Leda's brother, Giacomo, butler to the Marchese

44

and Marchesa dell'Orlando, Nicolò was appointed their private gondolier. He wore a livery of which he was intensely proud; his gondolier hat with its red ribbon came from a hatter who made the hats of the dandies among the gondoliers.

It was almost honorary work. Nicolò kept the gondola immaculate, took the Marchesa to Mass in the early morning, the Marchese to his club in the evening and fetched him; sometimes they dined out or went to the theatre, more particularly the opera. For the rest Nicolò was free to ply for anyone who would hire him and they were plentiful: he was skilful, reliable, and earned good money but, 'Che spreco!' mourned Leda. 'The waste! All those years at school and he speaks such beautiful English through Signora Marchesa who taught him, che Dio la benedica.'

The dell'Orlandos had known Nico, as they always called him, since he was seven when his uncle Giacomo had come into service with them. Nicolò had been encouraged to come to the palazzetto. He was an irresistible small boy, and mischievous. The Marchesa had particularly liked the mischief, for repeatedly he cut off his profusion of curls with his mother's scissors – to her grief – but the curls always grew again, as obstinate as Nicolò himself, and, though the Marchesa never said it, he brought balm to her heart. Her own young Eduardo had been killed in an accident when he had been given a sports car – they had no other children – and Nicolò could be truly dear. 'All the same, he's a little opportunist,' she told the Marchese. 'It amuses me how blatantly he tries to twist me round his finger.'

'And does twist you round his finger,' said the Marchese.

It had amused the Marchesa to teach him English, rather a stately English: Nicolò did not say 'yeah' or 'OK' unless he was with other gondoliers attempting pidgin

Americanisms, nor did he abbreviate, 'it's' for 'it is', 'I'd' for 'I would'. He had, too, learned manners, particularly from the Marchese, Eduardo Girolamo Francesco Enrico, eleventh Marchese dell'Orlando who, though physically small compared to the tall Marchesa, was proud, chivalrous and courteous even to a small boy.

His wife had been an English beauty and could still charm any boy or young man as Nicolò grew to be. She sympathized with him: 'I wouldn't want to be a white-collar worker shut in an office all day,' she told Leda when Leda had gone to her and opened her heart. As she said: 'Le ho detto tutto – I told her everything.'

'I should far rather be a gondolier.'

Leda sighed hopelessly. The Marchesa, always acute, heard the sigh and, putting her hand on Leda's, said gently, 'We mustn't force young people, Leda. They have to discover themselves in their own way and I have a feeling that Nico will make his mark.'

'What mark?' asked Leda.

The flat was Leda's world and she refused to give it up. 'I could afford you a far better one,' Nicolò often said. 'Up to date, convenient, modern.'

'But this is our home,' Leda insisted, and again, 'Your father was brought up here and your father's father.'

'No wonder it is so shabby.'

'It is ours.'

Off a small square and up sixty steps of a steep staircase, it was like a nest among the rooftops – unique, if Nicolò had only known it, with a view far over Venice, its roofs, chimney pots and nowadays, television aerials, away to where the dome of the Salute would glimmer in the sun, the moon, the starlight. More interesting, close at hand were the *altane*, the small, railed wooden terraces

Pippa had noticed, which made an extra room on the roofs of the large houses where, in the grander homes, visitors were entertained or, in Leda's world, women hung out their washing and dried their herbs and garlic. The flat had three rooms and a slit where Nicolò slept; the ceilings were low, some sloped, all freshly white-washed so that they reflected the light, grey on rainy days or lit with sun; at sunrise and sunset the walls turned pink.

The kitchen was its heart, a warm heart beating. There, washing was dried – Leda would not hang it across the street as the neighbours did so it hung politely on a rack over the cooking stove, an old-fashioned one but now, on Nicolò's insistence, run on oil. There was a smell of ironing and clothes airing, of polish, with a savoury aroma of cooking – Leda was an excellent cook and often went to help when the dell'Orlandos entertained – a smell accentuated by the plait of garlic and bunches of dried herbs hung over the stove and mingling with the scent of the geraniums she kept on the window-sill.

The table was covered with a bright oilcloth patterned with roses; the big dresser shone with copper pans and china and there was Leda's comfortable shabby armchair with her work-basket beside it. She could sit there looking at the television and hearing the echo of footsteps from the street below; if any came running up the stairway it was Nicolò.

Refusing to hang out her washing was not Leda's only pride: the third and largest room of the flat was her 'best room', kept for visitors and family celebrations, with a Turkey carpet, red velvet curtains, a three-piece suite and a table covered with knick-knacks. There were framed family photographs going back to grandfathers and grand-mothers, including Leda and her husband on their wedding day, many of Nicolò from a beautiful baby wearing only a vest to one taken last year in his gondolier uniform – Leda did not like that one.

There was a vase of plastic carnations and, seeming to preside, a huge picture of the Sacred Heart, Christ with golden hair and beard, a scarlet robe, pointing to his heart, open and surrounded by golden rays. There was also a piano, bought in the days when, to Leda's pride, Nicolò had been for a while a pupil at the Conservatorio di Musica di Venezia.

It was the piano that started contention. 'It is ridiculous to have a room that is hardly ever used.'

'*La gente per bene hanno sempre un salotto* – All respectable people have a best room.'

'Why can't I use it?'

Besides being a gondolier, Nicolò had a band which he took most seriously: he with his guitar – 'And my voice' – his friend Giovanni, Gianni, the accordionist and three other gondolier friends.

'But, Nico, a vulgar band!' mourned Leda.

'That's where we'll make money.'

'I'll believe it when I see it.'

'You'll see it when we really get started, but we can't start unless we can practise here.'

'But our piano!'

'Pianos are meant to be played. Besides, you can get rid of your old piano. Alfio has a keyboard.'

'*Che cosa diranno i vicini?* – What will the neighbours say?'

'Let them say.'

'Think of the noise! They'll put us out in the street.'

'Very well.' When Nicolò said, 'Very well,' he was dangerous. 'If we can't play here I'll go somewhere where we can.'

She knew he meant it and to justify herself – it was not only the neighbours but the whole street – 'It's his own band,' she boasted to them. 'Already they have engagements and I'll tell you a secret: he has been promised an engagement at the Imperiale Hotel at the Lido.'

48

There were still grumblings, shoutings up from the
street, bangings of protest on ceilings from the tenants on
the floor below. 'Always there is trouble with you,' Leda
shouted at him and now . . . 'A dancing girl I will not
have.'

'Mamma *mia*, I only want to show her I am respectable. You know the reputation of a gondolier.'

'I know the reputation of a dancing girl. No. A
thousand times no.'

'Very well, then,' said Nicolò. 'I'll ask Signora
Marchesa.'

'*Nicolò!* You wouldn't dare.'

'Signora Marchesa, may I ask you a question?'

'Of course, Nico, but I may not be able to answer
it.'

The Marchesa Marcia dell'Orlando had kept her tall
slenderness; her dark eyes were striking with her white
hair – she made no secret of her age, 'I am eighty.'

'But with never a wrinkle,' her husband said.

'Not yet.'

Hers was a noble face from a noble family. 'Marcia's
lineage is longer than mine,' he confessed. The forehead
was high, eyebrows straight, over eyes that had a level
and yet compassionate gaze – the people on the dell'
Orlando estates loved her. Her nose was straight too; she
had a beautiful mouth, tender, a little voluptuous, the lips
curved up at the corners as if she were going to laugh.
The Marchesa enjoyed life, 'Even now when I am old,
perhaps particularly now when I am old.'

'What is the question, Nico?'

'Signora Marchesa, am I respectable?'

She did not laugh; she had seen purpose in Nicolò's
eyes. 'Respectable? I hope you are.'

'But can you – how do you say? – prove it? I need it proved.'

'Only you can do that,' and, seeing the disappointment in his face, 'It's how you live, Nico.'

'But living takes such a long time. This is urgent. You see, Signora Marchesa, there is a girl.'

'Ah!' said the Marchesa.

'Not "Ah!". It is not what you think.'

'How can I think anything until you have told me?'

'There is,' said Nicolò, 'a Company of dancers that has come to Venice, an English company. They open tomorrow at La Fenice.'

'I know. The Midland Cities Ballet. We have had the brochure.' The Marchesa missed nothing of Venetian art life. 'We have taken tickets. Yes, they are giving, uncommonly, *The Tales of Hoffman*.'

'But only until the end of next week.' Ballet and ballets were beyond Nicolò's comprehension. 'We must act imperatively.'

'Act? For what?'

'For what I hope and pray.'

'Nico, tell me about this girl.'

'She is staying at the Pensione Benvenuto with many other girls.'

'The Skinners? Other girls? Then she is probably in the *corps de ballet*. That's like the chorus in an opera,' the Marchesa explained. 'Nico, where did you meet her?'

'I brought her from the station, she and some other ones, in my gondola. When we left the Grand Canal by the Rio Sansovino she asked me about the church.'

'Which church?'

'The little San Giuseppe.'

'Dear Saint Joseph. That was a good augury.'

'And last night in the restaurant . . . Signora Marchesa, you know Carlo's?'

'Of course.'

'I went in to play my guitar and sing with Gianni of my band. She was there and she recognized me, I am sure she did. Afterwards I took them home, she and her friends.'

'Other girls and boys?'

'Two older gentlemen and a lady not young, a senior lady. We did a little tour along the Grand Canal to see the moon on the water – to please the girl – it was a half-moon. They all seemed very fond of her.' He remembered the kiss. 'I can please her too. I know I can,' said Nicolò, 'but first I must be respectable. After we said goodnight, I asked one of the gentlemen for her name.'

'Did he give it to you?'

'He told me to go about my business, so that's what I did.' He laughed. 'I asked Carlo. He did not know her last name but she is called Pippa.'

'Pippa! And she is young.'

'Sixteen, seventeen. She has not been to Venice before. I think not to Italy.'

'Pippa,' the Marchesa said softly, and:

> 'The year's at the spring
> The day's at the morn . . .'

'What did you say?'

'Only – you are a lucky boy.'

Nicolò was startled. 'It's not what you think. She sang last night. She is most pretty when she sings.' Nicolò said it like a connoisseur – Which he probably is, thought the Marchesa. 'And she sings like a bird. I want that she sing in my band.'

The Marchesa said, 'Oh!' not 'Ah', but Nicolò swept on.

'You see why I must be respectable. I thought to take her home but Mamma will not receive her. "A show girl!" she says, just like that.'

'A ballet dancer, Nicolò, in a company like the Midland

Cities Ballet is not just a dancing girl. She is a highly trained serious artist, and you remember that.'

'Which is why I must be respectable. Oh, Signora Marchesa, please, please may I bring her here?'

'I must speak to the Signore Marchese.'

'There is not time. Besides, he always does what you say.' And Nicolò implored, '*Gentilissima* Marchesa. Please.'

'I should certainly like to see her but —'

'Tomorrow at four? A million, million thanks.' And in his fervour Nicolò kissed her hand.

'But . . . will she come?'

'I make her come,' said Nicolò.

'Signorina.'

The *corps* were having a few minutes' rest after a gruelling session for the courtesan scene in *The Tales of Hoffman*; they were sitting on the narrow benches at the sides of the rehearsal room watching while Angharad took Faye through her solo as Olympia, the doll. A few had slipped out for a glass of water, one or two lay flat on the floor.

'Signorina . . .'

Pippa looked up. It was one of the local stage hands. Now he was at her elbow whispering: 'I am Paulo. You . . . Signorina Pippa?'

'*Si.*'

'A young man he ask speak with you. È un bravo ragazzo – good fellow.'

The first thing Nicolò had heard as he stood at the stage door was the barcarolle, 'Belle nuit / Ô nuit d'amour'. He had sung it a thousand times, it was always given in the gondola-flotilla night concerts; he sang it, too, when bringing the Marchese back from a banquet, theatre or opera. 'Ô nuit d'amour'. Now it was being played on a piano – not a keyboard – but it seemed to make a link.

Nicolò had seen ballet on television, though Leda usually switched it off. It had seemed to him utter nonsense, the women elongated when they were on *pointe* as young men held them, turned them, carried them aloft all with waving, weaving arms and gestures. 'What rubbish,' he had said, though he liked it when the men danced alone with leaps, bounds, jumps high in the air, their feet making lightning changes; even he could see the virility and, 'That is something like dancing,' he said but now the stage doorkeeper was guarding it as if something sacred was going on upstairs, nor would he accept the note Nicolò had written or take a message.

With his usual stubbornness Nicolò had hung about outside, hoping to see someone he knew and, sure enough, one of the stage hands, Paulo, came out for a smoke. He whistled, then, 'Hi! Pauletto!'

'I don't know any good fellows,' Pippa told Paulo now.

'He know you. *Per favore*, Signorina. A little minute, not big,' and he measured two inches between his finger and thumb with a beguiling smile. These Italian men, thought Pippa. You can't resist them.

'He not eat you.'

'Where is he?'

'Outside.'

Paulo led the way to the little courtyard Pippa had seen. She had put on a light sweater over her leotard. 'Even if it's hot, cover up,' Angharad had said. 'You don't want a chill.' Her hair was in its usual knob with the old chiffon scarf, her face and neck still shining with sweat. For a moment she looked bizarre to Nicolò – Have I made a mistake? Then sense prevailed, I sweat in my gondola, but he had had no idea that dancing was hard work. Up

to now, Pippa had had a dream quality for him; now she
was not only real, she was akin.

'It's you.' The blue eyes smiled in pleased surprise.

'It is I, myself. *Buon giorno*, Signorina Pippa.'

'You know my name?'

'I found it out. I am Nicolò – Nico. How do you do?
That is what English people say to one another when they
are introduced. Now, Signorina . . .'

'We are rehearsing. I must hurry. What do you want?'

'That you should accept a so gracious invitation that I
bring you.'

'An invitation. For what?'

'To meet an old English lady in Venice.'

'Old? English? I don't want to meet any old English
ladies in Venice.'

'This one you do. Yes!' Nicolò was emphatic. 'She is
married to an Italian. She is a very great lady, the
Marchesa dell'Orlando.'

'Marchesa? But that's a title.'

'Yes. They are very noble. She asks you to come to
the Palazzetto dell'Orlando today at four o'clock. I think
your dancing is easily finished by then until evening. I
will come for you in my gondola.'

'But why should she ask me?'

'So many buts!' He smiled at her. His smile was even
more irresistible than Paulo's. 'She asks you because I ask
her. She is like my godmother.'

'So it's you who really asks me.' Pippa felt her heart
lift.

'Signorina, will you come?'

'Pippa.' It was Juliet's voice, faithful Juliet come to
look for her.

'I must go.'

'Please say first you will come.'

It sounded like an adventure and, Why not? thought
Pippa. What harm could there be in an old lady, especially

a *marchesa*? Pippa had never heard of a *marchesa* until this moment. Was she the same as a marchioness?

'Pippa! Pip-pa. Come *on!*'

'Say yes.'

'*Si*,' and Pippa fled.

VI

'What a beautiful gondola!'

The prow and stern were ornamented, the velvet cushions red not black. Nicolò – Nico – was waiting, not at the *pensione* steps below the lions but discreetly some yards down the *fondamenta*. He was dressed in a kind of livery, black trousers and bolero jacket which had buttons and epaulettes in gold, a crimson shirt and sash. His head was bare and the black of his curls had a sheen in the afternoon light. It was obviously an occasion.

Pippa had been uncertain what to wear. She had heard that to meet the Pope it was necessary to wear evening dress but that was obviously not suitable – in any case she had no evening clothes with her. In the end she chose the strawberry pink dress she had worn to Carlo's, white sandals, and brushed her hair vigorously. If she had known, nothing could have pleased the Marchesa more.

'Is this your gondola?'

'No, no.' When Nicolò laughed his teeth showed, beautifully even and white. 'It is the gondola of the dell' Orlandos. It has not changed for three hundred years except the cushions covered again. I keep it clean and polished.'

'You do?'

'Yes, I am private gondolier as well as public.'

'To the Marchesa?'

'And Signor Marchese. There is no gondola like it, or very few: if rich people have private boats now they are water-taxis.'

Pippa stroked the cushions. 'You're proud of it.'

'Certainly. Sometimes I even sleep in it unless it is very cold and wet and then I have to take everything, every least thing, and lock it away.' He slept there partly to get out of the flat, partly against thieves.

'Is stealing so bad?'

'They would take everything, the cushions, the cords, even my little lunch box of salami if I left anything in it, so I sleep here to save locking up. If you, Signorina, wear shoulder bag do not let it hang, as stupids do, keep your hand on it.'

In a few minutes they were in the Grand Canal. 'I love this great wide water-street.'

'Water-street?' Nicolò laughed then dropped into an imitation of a guide. 'All the world comes to Venice, all the great people. Popes, kings, princes, artists, poets like the Lord Byron. One of his ladies threw herself into the canal.'

'Why?'

'Because of love. Another poet, Robert Browning, he died here.'

'Didn't any of them live?'

'Dozens. There was a dancer like you. Taglioni.'

'Not like me. She was a great dancer.'

'So you will be too, now you have come to visit us. Wagner, the composer, wrote some of his music here,' but Pippa had given a small yawn. 'You do not like history?'

'I like nowadays.'

'The Marchesa says that now is also history . . . all is one. There was one name I remember too, Signorina.'

'Say Pippa.'

'As I am Nico. Pippa, who was Galileo?'

'Nico, didn't you ever go to school?'

'Of course, but I did not listen.'

'Galileo was a famous astronomer. He discovered that the world was round, not flat.'

57

'How did he do that?'
'By the stars.'
'The stars, yes, of course. We have a song,' and he sang:

'The world is a ball of wishes
Floating in bowl of stars . . .

'Pippa, I shall tell you a secret. I have a band, my own band and soon we shall be playing and singing at the Lido – at the Rotonda of the Imperiale Hotel – the most expensive. The Lido is where rich people come. They come in yachts, in their own planes. They come for the beaches and the hotels. I will take you to the Lido, Pippa.'
'You can have lidos and hotels,' said Pippa. 'I've come for Venice.'
'And here she is.'
They had turned off the Grand Canal into another of the myriad small waterways that led from it. There was quiet here, the *vaporetti* could not get down it and Nicolò had to handle the gondola carefully, sending his whistle ahead, or using his oar to push past a motor-boat. 'They do such damage, scraping the walls. There is war, Pippa, between the gondolas and the water-taxis.' They passed a barge tied up with a wonderful display of vegetables; people with baskets were buying. Another barge passed them, heaped with barrels and a goat loose on it. They rounded a corner into deeper quiet.

Both banks were lined with houses, not huddled together, most with slit windows as if they turned their backs on the canal, and had high walls showing a glimpse of gardens behind them: trees, fig and acacia, creepers, roses and wisteria hanging over the walls. All had steps going down to the water, some with gondola posts where private smart motor-boats were moored and heavy doors kept firmly shut. Very special people must live here, thought Pippa.

Nicolò looped a rope over one of the gondola posts of
a grey stone house, at first sight not large. 'Siamo arrivati.'
He went ashore and again held out a hand to help her.
'Don't be afraid. The *palazzetto* is not famous and in the
guide books, though Signor Marchese is the eleventh
marchese to live here – they are very quiet.'

He spoke at the intercom, a voice answered and after
a moment he could open the heavy doors. Pippa was
surprised when they stepped through: they were not in a
hall but an archway that tunnelled under the house; at its
end, she could see, through wrought-iron gates, finely
scrolled, what seemed to be an Italian garden of old walls,
stone-flagged paths, a tangle of flowers and, what she had
not seen in Venice, a cypress tree all in sunlight. 'La
Signora Marchesa loves her garden,' said Nicolò. 'Next
time, you must see it but now is no time. Come,' and he
led her to another door – there were several in the archway
– and pulled a bell rope. The bell jangled, breaking the
stillness; then the small door opened.

The man who stood there was unmistakably like
Nicolò, though plumper and bald, his skull shining and
brown. He wore black trousers, a striped linen jacket.
'My uncle, Giacomo.'

'*Buona sera*, Signorina.' He must be the butler, thought
Pippa. 'La Signora Marchesa is expecting you.' He, too,
spoke English. 'This way, please.'

They followed him into a vast room – it looked to her
as big as a ballroom – a room that made the title *palazzetto*
more than justified. At either end were windows so broad
and high that the room and its painted ceiling were flooded
with light and, on the polished floor, the sunlight made
brilliant patches. In the centre was a great chandelier, its
crystal glittering, too.

Along the white panelled walls, gilt scrolled with
candle sconces, were portraits of those other ten *marchesi*,
their wives and children, but they were so much a part of

the room that it did not look formal as with a picture gallery, while over one marble fireplace – there were two – hung the portrait of a young woman in a wide hat holding not a basket of roses but one of gardening tools and she was wearing a gardening apron. Pippa did not need to be told, it was the Marchesa.

The room was furnished with gilt chairs covered in brocade, narrow ormolu tables and cabinets, but it still looked empty. 'This', whispered Nicolò, 'is where I would like my band to practise,' but, 'Chut!' said Giacomo who had overheard. '*Basta* – enough.'

He opened one of the doors that led out of the room and stood aside. '*La signorina inglese*,' he announced.

It was a small sitting room but what Pippa saw beyond was a terrace above the garden and, over its balustrade, a fall of roses so abundant they hid the stone and ran up the side of the house, small creamy-white flowers and yellow buds. 'Oh!' breathed Pippa.

'Yes, they are a sight. I never tire of looking at them.' A tall old lady rose from her chair. 'I thought we would have tea out there.' She took Pippa's hand and drew her forward. 'So you are Pippa,' the voice was resonant, deep, 'but Nico did not tell me you were so pretty,' and Pippa found the wit to say, 'He didn't tell me you were so beautiful.'

'Then we are quits.' The Marchesa laughed.

The sitting room, its french windows opening on the terrace, was uncluttered; bookcases lined the walls, more books were heaped on a table, some with modern jackets. There were few ornaments, only bowls of flowers, Persian rugs on the tessellated floor, a boudoir grand piano, two or three comfortable chairs. 'We'll go on the terrace,' said the Marchesa. 'Come and sit down.'

Sitting in a wicker chair at a small table, 'I've never seen such roses,' Pippa said as she breathed their scent.

'All from a few bushes, but "Madame Alfred Carrière" is a generous rose.' It had not crossed Pippa's mind that roses had names. 'I'm glad you could come.'

'It was good of you to ask me. 'I . . .' She stumbled but she could not be nervous with this *marchesa*. 'I wasn't expecting anything like this could happen to me in Venice.'

'Perhaps that's why it has. Nico, ask Giacomo to bring tea. Being English, like me,' she said to Pippa, 'I assume you like tea. Now, tell me, what have you been doing in Venice?'

'Not much. You see, we have classes and rehearsals most of the day – there's only a short time between and tonight we have to be in the theatre by six. It's our première but I have been in cafés, and to St Mark's piazza and to a restaurant.'

'Nico said it was Carlo's. You couldn't do better but most foreigners don't know it.'

'It was our conductor, Pax Pemberton who knew it.'

'Ah, Pem! He would know. Yes, it will be good to meet him again. We avoid premières but we are coming to see you on Friday night.'

'Are you really?'

'I wouldn't miss it. And you are doing *The Tales of Hoffman*, one of my favourite ballets.'

'I'm only in the *corps*.'

'So I guessed but you have to start. One day . . .'

Giacomo brought tea, the kind of tea Pippa had only seen on television: a silver tray, china teapot and cups so thin they were almost transparent, silver spoons in the saucers; tiny sandwiches, little iced cakes, a plum cake. 'I hope you like Earl Grey.' The Marchesa had moved to the table to pour out and, seeing Pippa's blank look, 'It's a blend of Indian and China tea. We always drink it. Lemon or milk?'

Pippa had never had lemon in tea so said at once, 'Lemon, please,' and, 'What perfect cups!' she could not help adding.

'Yes. One of the pleasures in life is, I think, to drink good tea out of a fine cup,' and Pippa thought of her and Cynthia's mugs at the kitchen table. But then Cynthia does not have a Giacomo, she thought loyally, and there must be other servants.

'Not many,' the Marchesa would have told her. 'Not these days. A cleaning woman, a gardener, our dear cook who has been with us forty years and is now almost past it – and Leda, Nico's mother, comes in sometimes to help. We do keep a private gondolier – Nico – which is uncommon nowadays, but then we stay here all the year round except for August and Christmas when we go to our estate. Eduardo, my husband, does not like motorboats. He says they are noisy and stink.'

The Marchese arrived for tea. Pippa had expected him to be impressive, tall and noble like his wife, but he was a little man, agile and sprightly, though he had a shrivelled face – Pippa, to her astonishment, thought of a monkey. How could I? His hair, like the Marchesa's, was white – it looked silver in the afternoon light. His small brown eyes lip up when they saw Pippa.

'Eduardo, this is Pippa.'

'Delighted!' He took her hand and kissed it.

'She is in the Midland Cities Ballet at the opera house where we go tomorrow.'

'Splendid,' said the Marchese and, as he took his cup, 'You must tell me, my dear, about your work in the ballet.'

'He was really interested,' Pippa was to write to Cynthia, 'and he is the Marchese dell'Orlando, l'Ordine al Merito della Repubblica Italiana, Cavaliere di San Marco, Grand Chancellor of the Knights of Malta, Medaglia d'Oro', Nicolò had recited them for her, 'and goodness knows what else.'

'But we mustn't poach,' the Marchesa told him. 'Pippa is Nicolò's friend.'

'That scamp,' said the Marchese and laughed.

'Truly, and he says it is my duty, Pippa,' said the Marchesa, 'to tell you about him.'

'Present his credentials?' said the Marchese. As if Nico were an ambassador and I was a queen, thought Pippa.

'I promised him.' The Marchesa laughed too. 'He first came to us when he was seven years old with Giacomo. Pippa, I wish you could have seen him. When he was a little boy, you couldn't have resisted him.

'As we could not,' said the Marchese. 'He was an imp but he made us laugh.'

'Giacomo would not let him intrude but Nico has a talent for getting his own way as you will find when you know him better.' The Marchesa said 'when', not 'if' – As if I had no choice, thought Pippa but, come to that, she did not want a choice.

They told her about teaching Nicolò English. 'He speaks beautiful English,' said Pippa.

'But I'm afraid in an old-fashioned way, like me,' said the Marchesa. They had let him play on their piano – 'Not this one, the concert grand in the salon. Such a big piano for such a little boy' – gave him music lessons, sponsored him in the College of Music where he didn't last but, 'Somehow, I think, Nico is better untaught, music comes out of his fingers. His mother is a good wman but she i always trying to force him into the wrong pair of shoes. Poor Leda. He must take you to see her. You would be an education.'

'Me, an education!'

A clock in the room behind them chimed. Half past five, and Pippa cried, 'Oh, I must go. I am so sorry.'

'Nicolò will take you at once.' The Marchesa rang the bell on the tray. Nicolò appeared so promptly that he must have been waiting at the door.

The Marchese came with them to the archway. 'Next time you must see the garden.'

'Next time.' A surge of happiness filled Pippa. On impulse she kissed him.

Back in the sitting room, 'She is delightful,' the Marchese told the Marchesa.

'Yes. I'm glad she came but, Eddy, I don't usually encourage strangers, why did I, so easily, let her come?'

'The answer is simple, my dear, Nicolò asked you, but he has certainly picked a sweet and unpretentious girl. When I told her we should see her on Friday she impressed on me she was only in the *corps de ballet*, except they call them artists now, as she told me.'

'Artists, first artists, soloists, first soloists,' Pippa had said. 'Then, if we're good enough – and we have to be very good and lucky – principals.'

'She told me too, but I like the old names, *corps de ballet*, *coryphées*, ballerinas,' and it was not only in the *corps* that they saw Pippa dance.

She had told Juliet she was going for a walk. 'That was a long one,' Juliet said when, just in time, Pippa came breathless into the *corps* dressing room. 'I was coming to look for you.'

'Don't ever do that,' Pippa nearly said it but caught it back. 'That was dear of you,' she said instead.

'Has anything happened? You seem so excited,' but Pippa had disappeared into the bathroom.

VII

'I don't want this night ever again, thank you,' said Humphrey after the première. Weary and dispirited, the dancers had all left, but Humphrey, Robert and Angharad were in Humphrey's bare and cheerless office.

'I thought Italians were responsive,' said Robert.

'Well, they didn't respond tonight.'

The applause after the first act had been lukewarm; after the second act there were several empty seats but Angharad was steadfast. 'They did clap the barcarolle.'

'They shouldn't have. It was disgraceful. That young Pippa!'

'At least to have it clapped in Venice was something,' Angharad tried to say.

But Humphrey had staked so much on *The Tales of Hoffman*. 'I thought it would have been perfect for a Venetian audience, but none of it worked, none of it. Faye *simpered*!' he said in wrath. 'Jasper! That young man ought to have been a plumber for all he feels.'

'That's not fair.' Angharad was the first to defend her dancers. 'Just because he has an off night.'

'But dancing Hoffman he is *essential*. No. I made a mistake. It's probably too long and complicated a ballet but it *should* have worked. It should.'

The Tales of Hoffman is undoubtedly a long, complicated ballet as the long, complicated programme notes show:

The Tales open with a prologue in a tavern next to the opera house where Hoffman's present love, Stella, the

65

prima donna, is singing. It is a lively, bawdy scene taken at great pace and crowded with people – when Hoffman, poet, story-teller and perpetual lover, comes in; he has a quill pen and paper intending to write but he is at once besieged, especially by a party of students, to tell one of his stories, particularly of his loves. He is, though, dazed by drink and mimes that his love is now only for Stella, the amalgam of all his previous loves: a beauty, a courtesan and an innocent young girl.

The students persist and persuade Hoffman to tell of his three affairs. It is announced that the curtain is rising in the opera house, but most of the crowd and young men prefer to light their pipes, fill their glasses and listen to the tale of Hoffman's loves. The first love, of act one, is Olympia.

For the Company it was danced by Faye Richardson. 'I must say Faye is so attractive that everyone could fall in love with her,' said Humphrey.

An eccentric inventor, Spalanzani has invented a life-size mechanical doll. Hoffman, who is supposed to be studying science, is his pupil in Spalanzani's proper calling of scientist, and tells the young man of his beautiful daughter Olympia. Hoffman is puzzled because he cannot see what a daughter has to do with science but when he is left alone, he pulls back a mysterious curtain. His heart leaps as he sees a girl, whom he takes to be Spalanzani's daughter, fast asleep.

Niklaus, Hoffman's friend, companion and guide, arrives and makes fun of Hoffman's love, warning him of what he may find when he comes to know her better, but an itinerant optician, Coppelius – who is also Spalanzani's partner – comes in and sells Hoffman a pair of magic spectacles, which make him see what he wants to see, not what really is.

Spalanzani tells them he is giving a ball for Olympia's
début; he invites them and the scene changes to a ballroom
where guests in full Georgian costumes are arriving.

'I'd love to wear one of those,' said Pippa, looking at
Pearl's blue taffeta ruffles with a rose-bespangled bodice,
skirt and white wig, but as one of the gypsies in the
entertainment, Pippa had a ragged skirt and kerchief.

Olympia is brought in, attracting much attention. She
curtsies and sits in a special chair from which she can
answer questions, Spalanzani pressing invisible buttons.
He announces that she will sing an aria, 'Les oiseaux dans
la charmille' accompanied by a harp – she has a voice like
a flute.

It was Pippa, standing in the wings who sang for Faye;
she had to make the sound mechanical and as, every now
and then, the clockwork ran down, Spalanzani in panic
winding it up, the song had to be uneven – Pem had
coached Pippa endlessly.

Hoffman, in his magic spectacles, is too infatuated to
notice that Olympia is a doll and asks her to dance but she
is over-wound and dances furiously, faster and faster until
he cannot keep up with her and falls, breaking the spectacles. Coppelius rushes on; he has realized that Spalanzani
has cheated him over Olympia. He seizes her and breaks
her, holding an arm aloft.

Faye had to act here as a broken doll, which was
difficult to mime.

Olympia is carried away and Hoffman realizes Niklaus
is right: she is only a toy.
The second act is set in the *palazzo* of Giulietta, the

courtesan. The room is lined with mirrors and has a balcony overlooking a canal; there is a huge bed with draperies. Giulietta is giving a soirée.

As always in *The Tales of Hoffman*, Humphrey's direction was one of untrammelled bawdiness, but 'You should see it in London,' said Pearl. 'In the Midlands we have to be more proper.' All the same Pippa was startled to see boys, seven or eight to ten or eleven, brought in locally, fawning over the men who were mostly unbuttoned. Other courtesans titillate them while the Company's Maria Esslar of the flaunting good looks, as Giulietta, goes from one to another, which infuriates her current lover Schlemil and amuses Niklaus – Maurice Le Roy was a graceful dancer whose slight femininity gave no inkling of his strength.

'But he doesn't always control it,' Angharad worried. 'He's impetuous.'

It was here that Maurice and Maria danced the barcarolle; after its *pas de deux*, the traditional line of girls came on, Pippa among them. Though they wore the small tricorn hats, also traditional, half-masks and short seductive veils, their flounced skirts only came to the hips, the bodices were mere cups for breasts, leaving backs and midriffs bare. When the flounces were kicked up they showed legs up to the groin. 'More like the can-can than a barcarolle,' Pem objected.

'It suits the scene,' said Humphrey.

Giulietta, provocative, deliberately introduces Hoffman, who has been smitten with her, to Schlemil. There is play with an evil old magician, Dapertutto, who entices Giulietta with a diamond ring, but the price is Hoffman's reflection. He shows Hoffman a mirror, asks for the reflection and, in spite of Niklaus's entreaty, Hoffman swears that his love, his life and his reflection are all Giulietta's.

'How can anyone give away his reflection?' asked practical Zoë.
'It's a tale,' said Pippa. 'Angharad says you have to believe in magic. Watch Jasper. He makes you believe and, however silly, sympathize with everything Hoffman does.'

Dapertutto tells Hoffman he is too pale. Hoffman looks in the mirror again; it is blank. His reflection is gone. He curses his passion for Giulietta. Niklaus urges him to leave as the last guests are going. Then the music of the barcarolle is heard again. Giulietta goes to her room and signals to Hoffman, who demands the key from Schlemil. Schlemil draws his sword and challenges Hoffman. In the duel Schlemil is killed. Hoffman seizes the key and rushes to Giulietta's room but it is empty. As he stands bewildered he hears laughter beyond the balcony. He goes towards it; Giulietta is mocking him from a gondola where she lies in the arms of still another lover.

'If you had told me I would enjoy dancing Hoffman I wouldn't have believed you,' said Jasper, 'but I've almost come to like the silly bastard – at least he feels and, by God, I could fall in love with Maria's Giulietta myself.'
'Don't make the scene too strong,' Angharad cautioned him. 'Remember, it's only the second act – for the third you'll need all you've got. You have to put across a strength and tenderness that Hoffman hasn't shown before.'

The third act of the *Tales* is, by contrast, gentle. It takes place in the house of Crespel, a collector of musical instruments; his wife, now dead, had been a famous dancer and their daughter Antonia has inherited not only her

mother's talent but the disease that killed her. When the scene begins, Antonia is dancing; she cannot finish and sinks on to a sofa, exhausted.

Crespel rushes in and reproaches her because she has broken her promise not to dance again, but Antonia turns to the portrait of her mother that hangs in the room and tells her father, in mime, that she has to dance as only then can she feel close to her mother.

'Everything Isabelle does is exquisite – she completely has the feeling.' For once Angharad was more than satisfied.

Antonia tries to dance and fails. Crespel implores her to keep her word and also curses the influence of her new suitor, just declared, who is no other than Hoffman. Crespel has forbidden him the house, telling Franz, the servant, to keep watch, yet Hoffman and Niklaus steal in by the back door. Niklaus tries to restrain Hoffman; still he insists on seeing Antonia. In their love they dance an impassioned *pas de deux* but at the end she breaks down, to Hoffman's alarm and growing concern.

There is a long episode with a Doctor Miracle who assures Antonia she shall dance and should continue to break her promise. Looking at her mother's portrait Antonia prays for guidance. The portrait comes to life and the mother encourages the dying girl to dance, dancing with her.

Antonia falls exhausted, the portrait goes back into its frame. The frantic Hoffman carries Antonia to the sofa. Crespel comes in, aghast. Niklaus calls for a doctor but it is too late. She dies in Hoffman's arms.

The ballet has an important ending which comes back to the tavern where Hoffman has finished his story just as the last curtain comes down in the opera house next door. Niklaus proposes a toast to Stella, but Hoffman smashes the glass and vows that, though she is the epitome of his loves, he would rather find solace in wine. He sits drinking and when Stella arrives he does not recognize her. The tavern empties and he is left alone until Niklaus, transformed into the Spirit of Poetry in white draperies, a laurel wreath on his head, comes down the staircase and, in a tender *adage*, shows to a sadder and wiser Hoffman that love affairs are by the way; it is his art as a poet that matters. He blesses Hoffman and vanishes. Hoffman picks up the quill pen he had originally brought with him and begins to write.

'The ballet is badly planned,' Jasper at first complained to Angharad. 'The crisis comes in the middle, the end of the second act.'

'No, it doesn't,' Angharad contradicted. 'It comes at the very end, in the epilogue, and it is logical, as the best ballets are. We are seeing the development of a poet, and Offenbach knew exactly what he was doing. What is the second act for all its drama? Flummery, flamboyance and cynicism – it says something for Hoffman that he comes intact from that. The third act is curiously pure and Hoffman must reach a new height of emotion and show tenderness. Not easy for you I know' – Jasper excelled in vigour – 'but you have to match up to Isabelle. She may even make them cry.'

I should love to do that, thought Pippa, who was listening. At that moment she was sure she could but after the curtain had come down on the practically unattended last curtain call of the première – almost all the audience had left – the dancers were told to remain on stage, Humphrey wished to speak to them in what Pearl called 'The Inquest'.

It was harsh. 'Not one of you danced up,' he told

them. 'Except Callum who was splendid and, yes, you, Maria. For the rest of you I was disappointed and ashamed.'

'It was a rotten audience,' Jasper reminded him.

'I'm not talking of the audience but of you,' and, 'Where is Philippa Fane?'

It was the first time he had used her official name and Pippa, blissfully unaware that things were so wrong, warm and exhilarated, had a sudden cold premonition of fear. As the least of the Company, she was standing in the back row and had to make herself come forward and stand out. 'I – I'm here.'

'It's a pity you are here.' Humphrey was ruthless. 'Martha said you weren't ready and how right she was!'

'But . . . what did I do?'

'Ruined the barcarolle, that's all,' and Humphrey's wrath and disappointment broke – he had forgotten he was speaking to a teenage almost newcomer, and in front of the whole Company. 'Blatantly overdoing it, spoiling the affinity and the line. You didn't keep in line because you forgot about the others, didn't you?' and as Pippa could not answer he bullied, 'Didn't you?'

'I suppose I felt carried away. I – I was thinking about the dance.'

'You were not thinking about the dance. If you had been you would have known it was a chorus when the dancers must keep together and move as one. If you can't control your dancing and your bloody little feelings, you are no use to us in the *corps*. Now get out of my sight and all of you go home.' Then he added more quietly – he had command of himself again – 'There is no more we can do tonight. Tomorrow . . .' but Pippa had crept into the wings.

Juliet went after her, put an arm round her. 'It's just Humphrey,' she said.

'No, it's me.' Stunned and shamed as she was, Pippa

managed to say, 'Every word he said is true. I had better go.'

'We're all going.'

'I mean, back to Wolhampton.'

The dismay of that first night was not only because of the lack of audience response: in the second act a disaster had struck. Maurice Le Roy, as he danced Niklaus in a duo with Hoffman, saw that the evening was not going well, and put all his virility into the dance. Trying to match Jasper's speed as he went faster and faster, Maurice lost control, as Angharad had feared, and in one of his leaps hit a stalwart piece of scenery that sent him stumbling into the wings.

Hoffman had had to finish the duo alone. The act was in full swing, Niklaus should have been on stage; in a moment he was – but a different Niklaus. Callum, Maurice's understudy, without direction, not losing a moment, had changed coats with Maurice and before the audience had noticed – some of them did not notice until the end of the ballet – went straight into Maurice's place where, almost immediately, he had to dance the barcarolle with Maria. He could not have been quicker.

'Good lad,' said Humphrey.

'That's what training does,' Angharad told the girls afterwards. 'It's not only dancing. There has to be resourcefulness, and you were good, too.' Not one dancer or actor had faltered, though the small Italian boys had to be sharply ordered back as they scampered to see; nor did Pem and his orchestra stop or even slow down. 'That's training!'

Martha had taken Maurice to hospital for X-rays. No bones were broken. 'Thank God,' said Humphrey, back in his office where Angharad, Pem and Robert had anxiously waited. 'He has a badly sprained ankle. He won't be able to dance for at least a month or possibly in Milan but . . . what now?'

Callum had already shown that his was a totally different Niklaus from Maurice's, not gentle, persuasive, but virile, strong, propping up Hoffman's weakness. 'Different, but he'll bring a great deal to the part.'

'Except the poetry.' Humphrey ruffled his hair in perplexity. 'Callum cannot be the Spirit of Poetry. He looked ridiculous in those robes tonight – the crowning calamity. God! We'll have to think.'

'I have thought,' said Angharad and she was not downcast.

The girls had gone back to the *pensione* dispirited – no one had the heart to go out. 'I thought this first night would have been so wonderful and exciting, all of us keyed up,' said Jenny. 'What was the matter with everyone?'

'The matter was the audience, not us.' Constance showed her feelings by being cross.

'Yes, it was a thankless task.' Zoë, too, was put off. 'Italians are supposed to be quick – they were like lead and we have to meet them again tomorrow.'

'Tomorrow may be better.' Jenny was the Company optimist. 'We're doing *Bayadère* and *Checkmate*. Maybe it was the *Tales* they didn't like.'

'But it's so beautiful and so funny.'

'Everyone doesn't think so.'

'And the night after next we have to do it again. Oh dear! And what about poor Pippa?'

When a dancer is censured, almost always the others go out of their way to be sympathetic and kind but now, with Pippa, what was there to say? Any of them who had watched the barcarolle, and especially the seven girls who had danced it with her, knew Humphrey was right, more than justified.

At last, 'You were silly, that's all,' Juliet told her, with which the rest concurred. 'You can dance the barcarolle perfectly in mood as Humphrey has seen time after time,' but Pippa shook her head hopelessly and they went back to their own apprehensions until Pearl, most experienced of them, spoke.

'There are always nights like this. You can't expect eulogies all the time. Haven't you any faith in yourselves? Where's your pride?'

That arrested Pippa; in fact she felt Pearl was almost speaking directly to her. She had been more than proud of her dancing and it had brought her to this, yet Pearl spoke as if pride were good and if Pearl said so it must be true and, indeed, for a moment Pippa stiffened, but then, 'Even if it is true I have jeopardized it,' innocently, but she was sure now, fatally. 'You are no use in the *corps*,' Humphrey had said.

She went miserably to bed but not to sleep. What will Angharad say? She flinched when she thought of that. What will Cynthia? At the thought of Cynthia the tears did come and it was a wan, red-eyed Pippa who appeared in the morning.

'I'm sure Humphrey won't send you away.' Juliet tried to comfort her as they walked to the theatre next morning.

'He will. He'll put me out of the Company,' and, when they were in the theatre, her worst fears were confirmed.

Martha met them. 'Pippa, you're not to come into class. Go to the office at once.'

Humphrey had Angharad and Pem with him, which seemed ominous, but Pippa looked only at Humphrey.

'I'm sorry, terribly sorry that I spoiled things last night,'
and again she said, lacerating herself, 'Every word you
said was true. I don't know what got into me but I'll
never let it happen again.' 'If you give me another chance,'
hung in the air but she could not say it, sure now that it
would be useless. 'I can only say I'm sorry and go.'

She turned to the door but, 'Don't go yet,' said
Humphrey. 'Angharad has something to say to you.' And
he did not sound in the least cross.

He and Angharad had been in the office since nine.
Humphrey was happier this morning. The reviews had
been more reserved than bad:

> The Company had not quite settled into
> this demanding ballet but obviously grew
> on the audience . . .

> A new and virile Company not quite on
> its form . . .

And Angharad argued, 'The house wasn't all that lukewarm after the second act.' The whole Company seemed
shaken into life after the débâcle. The papers had picked
out Isabelle and Maria, particularly Maria, and one had
gone further:

> The audience was not very intelligent last
> night. The Midland Cities Ballet and their
> Tales of Hoffman must be seen.

Angharad, too, had had a little private sop from Andrea
Strozzi, the oldest critic and a true connoisseur of ballet.
'Who was the girl, second from the left in the barcarolle?
She was one of the gypsies too.'

'Philippa Fane, our youngest. She's only seventeen.'

'You should watch her.'

'I am watching,' Angharad had said and, now, 'The *Osservatore* – it's an important paper – has a warm word for Callum.'

'He was splendid,' Humphrey was cheered, 'but Callum's no Muse. Then what to do? Angharad, you said you had thought. Then tell me, what are we going to do about this changed Spirit of Poetry?'

'It isn't really my place,' said Angharad, 'but I'd like to tell you. Before I do I should like Pem to be here.'

Humphrey raised his eyebrows. 'That sounds very radical.'

'It is. I'll call him.'

Pem was in the theatre and came.

'Well, Angharad. Who have you in mind for the Spirit of Poetry? Who?'

'Pippa,' said Angharad.

'*Pippa!* After last night?' Humphrey was aghast.

'Particularly after last night. That was a valuable lesson, Humphrey, and I'm glad you made it sharp. I know you'll find she has learnt it.'

'She showed off last night,' Pem put in.

'No, she tried too hard, that's all.'

'By God she did,' said Humphrey.

'Now she knows better – and she'll temper herself and, Humphrey, do you know what I think?'

'I'm trying to understand what you think.'

'If she had been dancing the barcarolle alone last night she would have brought it off. Admit!'

'True,' Pem pondered. 'She just didn't fit in with the other girls.'

'She's got to,' Humphrey was firm. 'One more try in rehearsal but I'm not going to risk it on stage again.'

'Pity,' said Angharad, 'when I'm asking you to take a far greater risk.'

'I should say so, that little chit as the Spirit of Poetry.'

'She isn't a chit and she's just at the point . . .' For a

77

moment Angharad was sidetracked. She closed her eyes, back in yesterday evening when Pippa had come in for Martha's warming up class and had passed Angharad who stopped her. 'You look sun-flushed.' The girl had never looked more lovely – lovely, beginning to be luscious, Angharad had thought. The petal skin had taken on a peach glow, the brown hair was already touched by the sun, the blue eyes were brilliant as if she had a fever. Angharad had reached out and touched Pippa's cheek lightly, deliberately lightly, with her finger. 'Do you like Venice so much?'

'I love it. I *love* it.'

God help me, Angharad had prayed and managed to say, 'Too much sun can be dangerous. You might get sunstroke.'

'I think I have.' Pippa had laughed and gone on to her class.

I should never have taken notice of her again. Angharad knew that but this was a matter of dancing. I must. I must try and keep things separate, and she said aloud, 'I know she can dance the Spirit of Poetry – if you'll give her the chance.'

'Why not?' said Pem.

'Apart from everything else, she's a girl.'

'So were all the muses, young, consecrated, like Pippa. In the opera of the *Tales*, Niklaus is always sung by a girl. Of course Pippa could not dance Niklaus.'

'You mean divide the role?'

'Yes. To have Niklaus turn into the Spirit of Poetry is logical but not absolutely necessary. She could be a character in her own right, detached.'

'That isn't in the ballet,' Pem pointed out.

'I know it wouldn't be traditional but tradition isn't sacred and I would go further,' Angharad challenged them. 'I would have the Spirit all through the ballet.'

'All *through*! But how?'

'In the first act when the guests, with Olympia and Spalanzani, have gone to supper and Hoffman and Niklaus are left alone, she appears. Hoffman welcomes her with open arms and they begin to dance together – Pem, you could repeat a little of the waltz for that – but Olympia comes in, Hoffman sees her, and straight away discards his muse.

'For the second act she again appears. Niklaus welcomes her and leads her to Hoffman but he has eyes only for Giulietta.'

'And the third?'

'She comes when Hoffman is grieving for Antonia. She tries to console him but he is wrapped in grief and she goes away. In the epilogue she comes down the staircase as in the *Tales* except that you, Humphrey, would have to adapt the solo for her. You could use the same music. This time Hoffman embraces her, they dance. This would need extra music. Then he begins under her direction to write.'

There was a silence until Humphrey said slowly, 'It could be.'

'It certainly is a break with tradition,' said Pem. 'But, as Angharad says, why not? I like the idea – actually it is more logical. I've always thought Niklaus turning into a spirit was a bit corny.'

'But could we do it in the time?' Humphrey was half caught up.

'We're doing the double bill tonight so we have two days and Pippa is quick and she's so devoted. Humphrey, she never takes her eyes off the principals when they're dancing.' Angharad had calculated it all. 'As I said, it would not need any extra music apart from the *pas de deux* at the end and extending the waltz, also for Antonia's death. We should have to rehearse the crowd scenes again, just a little.'

It grew more and more convincing.

Pem said, 'I believe Pippa could do the Spirit. She is so light, ethereal, at the same time alive and enticing. Angharad, you're clever.'

'I happen to believe in Pippa's talent and this chance seems to be made for her. Let's send for her and let her cut class.'

This time Humphrey had not demurred.

'We'll need the principals and Callum,' but when Pem had gone he said, 'Angharad, I think you're becoming obsessed with this girl.'

Angharad's head came up, she looked Humphrey in the eyes. 'Yes, perhaps I am, but when you find a dancer as promising, isn't it exciting? They thought she was remarkable at school, now she's blossoming.'

Humphrey did not answer.

'Andrea Strozzi noticed her,' but Humphrey was not to be evaded.

'For once, I wasn't talking about dancing,' he said.

VIII

'After all, that Thursday I had dreaded so much turned out to be my lucky day,' Pippa said afterwards.

'Sit down, Pippa,' Angharad had said. 'We want to talk to you. It's about *The Tales of Hoffman*. By now you should know it by heart. Do you think you do?'

'Yes.' Pippa was certain of that, but what was coming now?

'Of course, Maurice's accident has brought changes,' said Humphrey. 'Callum, I have confirmed, will dance Niklaus.'

'I'm glad.'

'But . . .'

'But?' Pippa was puzzled.

'It's concerning the Spirit of Poetry who comes down the great staircase in the epilogue. Remember?'

'Maurice again.' Pippa nodded.

'Maurice could do it, he had that quality, but Callum can't. He's too vigorous and masculine. So . . .'

'So?' Puzzled, Pippa looked from one to the other. They were smiling.

'I think you'd like to tell her, Angharad,' and Angharad said, 'There is going to be a new Spirit of Poetry who will not only be in the epilogue but in all three acts. Humphrey has created the part and it's now for a girl. You.'

'*Me?*' Pippa's eyes were wide with incredulity. 'Me!'

'If you can be very quick, very adaptable and will work hard. We have just two days.'

'But . . . after last night?'

'We'll forget last night,' Humphrey said. 'Don't think about it again.'

'No, forgive me, Humphrey,' Angharad contradicted him, 'Always think about it, Pippa. Perhaps it was the most valuable thing that ever happened to you, but now let's concentrate on the Spirit of Poetry,' and Angharad went on as if it were already a matter of fact. 'You will come out of the gypsy quartet. Jenny can take your place.'

'With quick changes you can still do the barcarolle,' said Humphrey, which was generous of him. 'Now go and ask Martha to let you warm up, then straight to the rehearsal room.'

'Wait, Humphrey, just a word.' Angharad spoke quickly. 'Pippa, the Spirit of Poetry is a muse from the old Greek myths. She is inspiration so she has to be ethereal, at the same time lively – she can nag a poet. You will wear a soft white Greek tunic caught under the breasts with a silver cord, silver shoes. You will be on *pointe.*' Pippa's eyes had begun to glow. 'From your shoulders there will be gauzy draperies and you will have a small wreath of laurel in your hair. There is more mime than dancing, but in the epilogue Humphrey is writing a lovely tender little solo especially for you.'

'Especially for me!'

'Well?' asked Humphrey. 'It's a big chance for you. Would you like to try?'

'Yes. Oh, yes.'

'Good. Go and get ready.' But when Angharad came out of the office, Pippa was standing against the wall.

'Humphrey told you to get ready. What are you doing?'

'Trying to believe it,' said Pippa and again, 'After last night it can't be true.'

For a brief moment she thought Angharad was going to put an arm round her but Angharad only said,

'We can't make it begin to be true if you don't go and change.'

'I didn't dream what it would be like dancing with Jasper and Faye, doing the mime with Giulietta,' Pippa told Juliet. 'I know now why they are principals. It does something to your dancing,' but she had a moment of fear: 'Last night the audience didn't seem to like even them.' She had not been told of the reviews. It suddenly seemed too daunting to dance her first named part, it could be called a début, in the face of an indifferent audience. She tried to say something of this to Angharad: 'If they don't like me,' she quailed, 'what can I do?'

'What the others do, as I am sure they will do every night. *Make* them like you.'

Humphrey left most of it to Angharad but every now and again he would come up to the rehearsal room to watch, making a little alteration, each time enhancing. 'Dance *into* it, Pippa. You're still outside it.' Towards the end of the long session he was still, sitting the wrong way round on his chair, his chin resting on the back of it, his eyes taking in every movement. Jasper's, Callum's, Maria's but chiefly Pippa's.

At last, 'I think, Humphrey, that's enough for now,' said Angharad.

It was two o'clock and, 'A good beginning,' said Humphrey.

'Pippa,' Angharad stayed her for a moment, 'I want you to get something to eat now, not just coffee, then rest, preferably on your bed. I'll see you again for your solo at half past four, just for an hour. You have to be ready for the performance tonight. Now eat, rest.'

Pippa went straight to the piazza and Florian's where she ate a mammoth sandwich. 'Italian sandwiches are not at all like English ones,' she had written to Cynthia. 'Crusty stick bread, butter with smoked ham or salami', and at Florian's she tried out her Italian. '*Panino prosciutto.*'

'The signorina speaks Italian!' said the flattering waiter.

There had had to be a pause during the morning session when Bertha came from the wardrobe to try on the dress she had already cut and tacked – she knew Pippa's measurements. For the material she had been forced to compromise on a fine silk: 'Soft but I am afraid it will cling – you will wear nothing under it except your briefs.'

She pinned on the draperies as the shoe lady came with the *pointe* shoes. 'We shall have to paint them. I can't get silver ones.'

It was an interruption, 'But that's when it began to be real,' Pippa told Juliet.

Juliet had come to join her at Florian's. She had heard the news – everyone had heard the news – and she was glowing. 'So here's where you are. I guessed so.'

Pippa beckoned the waiter. 'What will you have? Orange? A cappuccino?' And as Juliet chose a cappuccino, 'Have a sandwich or a cake.'

'Pippa. Remember the cost!'

'I really do have heaps of money now,' said Pippa, 'I've been promoted.'

'This brings problems,' Humphrey had told Angharad. 'Here is Pippa, not been with us a year and just an artist. Now she is taking what is a solo part – one must be fair to her.'

'Then make her a soloist!' said Angharad and, at the end of the long rehearsal, Pippa was on her way downstairs when Humphrey came out of his office.

'Pippa, I was coming to find you. Come in here for a moment.'

'I'm not very tidy.'

'I don't expect you to be, Angharad is working you hard. Sit down and rest your legs,' which Pippa was only too glad to do. She ached. 'I have to talk to you.'

'Am I doing something wrong?'

She was still nervous and knew how closely Humphrey had watched, but he was saying, 'You realize, don't you, Pippa, that this will bring you promotion.'

'Promotion?'

'And more pay.'

'I hadn't thought about it. I was just – so happy.'

'It goes with the job.'

Pippa did not think dancing should be called a job; it had always been impressed on her that it was a career but if Humphrey Blair said it . . . 'You mean I could be a first artist?'

'More than that. If this comes off, and I believe it will, I'm making you a soloist.'

'A soloist!' Pippa had almost fallen off her chair and now, at Florian's, 'You can have ten cappuccinos, ten cakes,' and she told Juliet what Humphrey had done.

'Well! Blow me down!' said Juliet. 'I knew you wouldn't stay with us *hoi polloi* for long but not even first artist, straight into soloist! That *is* something and I'm glad for you. You deserve it.'

And to think I called Juliet jealous, thought Pippa.

'How did it go?' Juliet was asking.

Pippa paused. She was puzzled. At the end of the session Angharad had said, 'If you can keep this up, I think it will be really good,' and, in her relief, Pippa had been moved to give her a grateful hug. Angharad had fended her off at once. 'We don't want to get all emotional,' she had said, her voice oddly crisp. 'Run along now like a good child,' but Pippa saw she had gone red. She's angry, she thought. Perhaps she's one of those people who don't like to be touched, and blushed for herself.

Now, 'I'd like to walk about a bit,' she said.

'You ought to rest.' Juliet echoed Angharad.

'If I do, I'll just go on dancing in my head.' Pippa was no longer worn or wan: she looked as fresh as if she had been given some elixir of life – as perhaps she had. 'Let's look at the shops.'

The piazza was crowded as usual but most of the people were on the square; the arcades along the shop-fronts were not as full.

Juliet, who loved clothes, gave envious 'ohs' and 'ahs' at the perfection and elegance of a simple-looking dress, at the colours of the scarves, pure silk, at hats, shoes. There were special shops for table linen, embroidered blouses, handkerchiefs, others for umbrellas and gloves. 'I can buy Cynthia *two* pairs of gloves now,' said Pippa. A sports shop had beautiful sports clothes, racquets, golf clubs, swimming and diving gear. There were camera and video shops, toys. Pippa paused to look at a pale blue teddy bear revolving on a stand, reminding her of the pierrot on the way to Carlo's. They strolled, looked, the sun dazzling outside, but it was cool here.

They came to a jeweller's; the windows were protected with a gold mesh, but behind it they could see a glittering display: necklaces, bracelets, bangles, rings, earrings, watches. There were no price tags on them, 'Which means they're expensive,' said Juliet. 'Fratelli Bastonello' said the gold and green sign above the entrance. 'Better come away,' said Juliet.

'No. Let's go in.' Pippa was in a daredevil mood. 'Let's pretend we want to buy a souvenir.'

'Costing five hundred pounds!' Juliet was beginning to join in. Her gaze had fallen on a small pink figurine. 'We'll ask to see some coral. Italy is famous for coral.'

It was a small shop but so elegant that they were immediately conscious of their casual clothes, jeans, sweatshirts, sandals. There were only two showcases, an impressive-looking safe on one of the green and gold striped walls, which had sconces with crystal drops that shone in the discreet light; there were hand spotlights on the glass counter tops. The carpet was so thick their feet made no sound. The inlaid chairs had cream velvet seats. 'It looks terribly expensive,' said Juliet.

'Yes. We shouldn't have come in,' but the shopkeeper – or was he the proprietor? – in his black coat, striped trousers, grey waistcoat, immaculate shirt, pearl tie-pin and gold ring had come forward smiling.

'*Buona sera*, Signorine,' and he said in English, 'What can I do for you?'

'Nothing, I'm afraid.' Pippa felt she could not go on 'cheating' as she felt it. 'Probably we can't buy anything.'

'But we'd like to look.' Juliet had recovered herself. 'May we?'

'Certainly, Signorina. It will be a pleasure.'

'Have you any coral?'

How silly, thought Pippa, we know you have. There's some in the window, but he brought out a heart-shaped velvet stand with an array of delicate and deeper pink. 'These are some of our brooches set in silver or gold, some with diamonds. We have earrings to match, necklaces, rings.'

Juliet made little noises of admiration, but Pippa was not listening. She had seen, in the showcase, a pendant lying by itself on a thin gold chain, a single stone, cut flat, oval, perhaps an inch wide and shimmering with a lustre that held a sheen of faint green, or was it gold? Almost like an opal but it was not an opal, she felt sure. It had a quieter lustre, more delicate and, 'What stone is that?' she asked.

'Ah! The signorina has an eye! It is a moonstone, a very fine one. We do not often see one as large.' He took it out of the showcase, laid it on the counter and turned a spotlight on to it; at once the sheen sank to a glimmer.

'See, it does not like the brilliant light. Like the moon it shines brighter in subdued light. There is nothing flashing about this jewel, it is not a show-off so it is for connoisseurs like yourself.' And he put it into her hand.

It felt cool, polished, a jewel! Up to now Pippa had not taken in the full meaning of the word – jewels had not come within her and Cynthia's compass, though she had admired the Marchesa's rings. Jewel: a rare word, a precious stone, moonstone as if it had been mined on the moon. Suddenly her whole heart yearned for it and, 'How much?' she found herself asking.

'Fortunately moonstones are not usually of much value but this one is a rare, so six hundred thousand lire.'

'Six hundred thousand . . .' It sounded an enormous sum but, 'That is three hundred pounds. For you, Signorina, shall we say two hundred and seventy-five.'

Pippa put it back on the counter.

'Signorina Pippa.' It was a cheerful and delighted voice and into the shop came Nicolò. He was not dressed in his gondolier clothes; he was wearing linen trousers, espadrilles, a short-sleeved cotton jersey, primrose-coloured that set off his hair. Zoë had been right on that journey from the station, Nicolò was a true dude. He still wore his gold bangle and gold earrings. He looked a more than presentable young man and, 'Introduce me,' prodded Juliet. Pippa had thought she would certainly remember the mass of curls but evidently not – perhaps she had not really looked at him and for her he had been part of the landscape.

'Juliet, this is Nicolò. Juliet is in our Company,' Pippa explained.

'So!' Nicoló bowed. 'And is Signor Bastonello robbing you? They are all sharks in the shops on the piazza, swallowing all the poor little fishes, hey, Roberto?'

'I wish he could,' Juliet said. 'He has some lovely coral, but he knows we're only looking.'

'Yes, and look at this, Nico.' The moonstone was still on the counter and Pippa said, 'Now I've seen that I don't want to look at anything else, ever.'

In Italian Signor Roberto was explaining to Nicolò what the pendant was. 'Moonstone,' said Nicolò and echoed Pippa's thought, 'It must have come out of the moon.'

Juliet looked at the two heads, dark and gold-brown bent over the counter and, What a pair, she thought.

'You like it?' he said to Pippa of the pendant.

'I'd give the world for it, but I haven't the world.'

Nicolò spoke again in Italian to Signor Roberto who answered but spread his hands helplessly. 'If you ladies compare my prices with London, Paris or New York . . .'

Pippa had to smile at the thought of her and Juliet comparing prices. 'I've never been to Paris or New York. I have been to London but, of course, not into a jeweller's shop. It's not your prices, Signor. It's ours . . .' and Signor Roberto regretfully put the pendant back in the showcase.

Juliet turned to go but Nicolò followed her and put a restraining hand on her arm. 'A little moment, Signorina Juliet. Will you and Pippa not take a drink with me, or is it English tea you like? There is a good small café on the waterfront.'

They were in the doorway. Pippa was saying goodbye to Signor Roberto. 'When you marry a millionaire,' he was saying, 'and I am sure you will marry a millionaire, Signorina, come back and see Signor Roberto again.'

'A little drink? You would like?'

'Very much, but Pippa has a rehearsal at half past four.'

'You take good care of your little friend. *Brava!*' He put his arm round Juliet's shoulder and hugged her.

Across the piazza, Angharad, who was going to La Fenice, saw them. Always astute she recognized Nicolò.

'We must fly,' said Juliet and called, 'Pippa.'

'I get you a gondola, free.'

'We'll be quicker if we run.'

'*Ciao*,' Nicolò called after them.

'*Ciao!*' they called back, feeling really Italian.

'So all this time you've known this young man and never told me a word!' said Juliet in the dressing room. 'You're a deep one!' but she sounded glad and relieved. Why should she be relieved? Then she said, 'I thought you had no eyes for anyone but Angharad.'

'They're in different worlds,' Pippa could have said. Instead, 'I never met him till I came to Venice.'

'But how could you meet him? There hasn't been time. Don't be so mysterious.'

'It's not mysterious. You've met him too.'

'I certainly haven't. I'd remember it. He's gorgeous.'

'Yes,' said Pippa. 'He's the gondolier who brought us from the station.'

'A *gondolier!*' The house of cards Juliet had been building for Pippa tumbled down. 'Oh, Pippa! *No*, Pippa.'

'I don't want you to get over-tired,' Angharad said when her afternoon session with Pippa had ended. 'Perhaps it would be best if you didn't dance tonight.'

'But . . . I must.'

'We can easily cover up for you.' But Pippa was in obvious dismay.

She especially loved *La Bayadère*, holding her *arabesque* then coming down the ramp. 'Oh, Angharad, please. Dancing never makes me tired.'

'Till afterwards.' Yet Angharad had to give in to that eagerness. 'Very well, then.'

Luck was still with Pippa that night, or was it the specialist coaching with Angharad and Humphrey? Or, as she had told Juliet, dancing with the principals? But Pippa knew she danced in both ballets as she had not danced before. 'You *are* in form,' said Humphrey.

He, too, felt in better luck: the audience, the whole performance, was different; the house full, the clapping whole-hearted. 'Almost I begin to hope,' he told Pem.

They all went to bed exhilarated. Then why, in the morning, did everything, to Pippa, seem so flat and at rehearsal she herself so listless? 'I was better yesterday,' she said to Jasper.

'Cheer up,' said Jasper. 'It often happens – after the first euphoria you get a second more sober wind and then comes the slog.'

But Pippa had heard Humphrey say to Angharad, 'I hope to heaven you haven't brought her on too soon,' and, 'There isn't time for slog,' she said in despair.

Angharad was steady. 'Jasper's quite right. This is perfectly normal.' She did not say, 'I shouldn't have let you dance last night,' only, 'You've worked too hard. You can't do any more to it at the moment so we'll leave it for now. Go and sit in the sun for a while then go back to the *pensione* and lie down. Don't think about dancing. Think of something nice.'

Something nice! Even Pippa's loved piazza, her sandwich and cappuccino, did not calm her. 'I'll never get through tonight. I'll let them down again.' Her nerves were in shreds. 'I wish Juliet were here.' Juliet had been called to go through the part of Giulietta, 'Because one never knows,' said Angharad. Suddenly Pippa could not bear the sun, the music, the crowds of people any more. I'll go and look at the moonstone, she resolved. Though you can't own something, mysteriously you have it for always and take it with you as a talisman, and I need a talisman. I'm sure Signor Roberto won't mind.

Signor Roberto was not in his shop, only a woman dressed in black with pearls and a perfect makeup. 'Good afternoon, Signora' – Pippa was sure she was a *signora* – 'I came in yesterday. May I look at the moonstone pendant again?'

'Signorina, it is sold.' Pippa saw that the place in the showcase was empty.

'When?'

'Yesterday afternoon.'

The desolation of the whole day suddenly seemed too much. Pippa burst into tears.

'My dear, did you like it so much?'

Pippa nodded. She could not speak and, blindly, found her way to the shop door.

She could not cry in broad daylight and she pushed through the crowd to go into the Basilica.

At the main entrance her attention was caught by a man barring the way – Was he an usher, she wondered – but he was barring a party from coming in; the men had no shirts on, the women were in shorts or low-necked sundresses, some with only a strap, showing bare legs, arms, necks, almost bosoms. They argued fiercely but he was adamant and, oddly enough, instilled a new feeling of respect: the men put on jackets, the women borrowed scarves and skirts.

Pippa went in. Unaccountably, as she felt now, she had not been in the Basilica before. Somehow, few of the dancers wanted to see the sights – but at once, instinctively, she knew this was not just a sight: 'Well, it's the most magical and mystical of churches,' the Marchesa was to tell her. 'If you give yourself time to realize it. Most people don't, poor things.'

She found herself propelled by the press of people to

go around the Pala d'Oro, the famous screen of gold with its panels of jewels that stood behind the high altar. The floor was uneven; under the moving feet she saw patterns. There was the smell of warm bodies, of the slight dampness of stone and marble, a scent of incense – a faint haze of it hung in the air high above. The tourists were a little hushed, though there was a continuous clicking of cameras and the loud voices of guides informing their groups. They shouldn't do that in here, Pippa thought, though why she minded she did not know. She had never heard the word sanctity.

As she extricated herself from the queue and looked round, she had the impression of dim spaces, side chapels with altars, pillars and galleries, all with carved figures and gleams of gold, but she was not looking at the Basilica and its treasures; she was watching the people.

There were some who did not stare and look but went at once to kneel and pray; some seemed to be in groups – she saw a bevy of Japanese. They must be pilgrims, she guessed. There were, too, women old and young, obviously locals, who flumped their full baskets and plastic bags down, knelt and prayed. Some of the younger ones had children, probably fetched from school – Venetian children all seemed to be well dressed. A few of them were allowed to light candles.

Now that her eyes had grown accustomed, she saw the great church was alive with glinting light, a flickering of candles beside the altars of some of the chapels – only the sanctuary lamp on its jewelled holder beside the high altar was steady. The Basilica was, too, full of murmurings, people were praying by the candlestands and she watched as coins and small notes were dropped into the money boxes; then hands held the taper, lit from another candle; for a moment faces were illuminated, often the lips moving in prayer.

All those candles are wishes or hopes, she thought,

perhaps for somebody ill or dying, or who was in trouble, or had had a dreadful blow; or perhaps they were for a baby being born or, trivial by comparison, success in passing an exam. And I thought mine was the only worry in the world! thought Pippa. She was moved to go to a stand, putting in not her small money but a ten-thousand-lire note, five pounds. As she took the candle and lit it, the warm breath of the myriad others was in her face; she seemed to carry that warmth with her as she knelt in a pew. 'Please. *Please!*' As the candle warmth went up it seemed to carry hundreds of 'pleases' up too, mingling with the traces of incense. Somewhere she had heard that frankincense was the symbol of prayer; there were centuries of incense here.

That morning she had had no hope; now a curious confidence was in her. She wondered what Cynthia would say if she could see what she, Pippa, was doing now? Probably, tolerant Cynthia would say, 'By all means do it, darling, if it makes you feel better.'

'I don't feel better. I am better.' As proof of that a common-sense call came: 'Go back to the *pensione* and do as Angharad said. Lie down until it is time for class.'

When Juliet came into their bedroom she found Pippa on her bed, peacefully asleep.

IX

There is no more stirring moment for dancers than when the curtain goes up for a performance; no matter how accustomed they are, each time they hear the familiar smooth *shrr* of the rise they are keyed up, ready and going into action with hardly time for a glance at the audience, yet they are conscious of them. Pippa, though her entrance as the Spirit of Poetry came far later, still chose, after the prologue, to wait backstage and, 'If you lean against anything or sit on one of those old benches I'll wring your neck,' Bertha told her. 'Don't even touch anything with your hands. That white will show every mark.'

It seemed an interminable wait while Jasper/Hoffman went through his scenes with Humphrey/Spalanzani, then with Callum/Niklaus and Coppelius; she had to wait for the ball and the beginning of the waltz when at last she could come on, the guests making room for her. She circled Hoffman on *pointe*, seemed about to come into his embrace, eluded him, then gave in to his entreaty and danced with him. There was a moment when, his arms round her, she put her hands each side of his face, looking into his eyes; it was a moment of mutual rapture – almost she was going to kiss him. 'The kiss of inspiration,' Angharad had told her, 'which is your poetic gift to him,' but he looked past her, saw Olympia again and left so abruptly that Pippa was sent spinning away on her *pointes* in a whirl of *déboulés* until she vanished.

'Well done,' said Angharad from the wings.

The evening went, 'Like a dream,' said Humphrey but Pippa had no time to dream, each scene seemed to come a little better than the last. She had a quick change for the barcarolle, Bertha helping her into the green and gold skirt and top, the little tricorn hat and veil, carefully keeping the white dress ready – it was to go on again in a few minutes. For the barcarolle Pippa had to school herself to be in trim with the others – she was between Constance and Jenny – and become saucy, bold, as far removed from the Spirit of Poetry as she could be. 'Don't overdo it, girls,' Humphrey had said, perhaps to caution Pippa. 'As you know it can run away with you.'

It ran away with the audience. The girls had to dance it again.

To Pippa the ballet went quickly until she reached the moment in the epilogue when she had to come down the staircase of the empty tavern where Hoffman was sitting forlornly alone. 'Come slowly, make your full effect,' Angharad had told her. 'Pem will take the time from you.' Then Pippa went into the solo that roused Hoffman and brought him to her in the *pas de deux* that was almost the end of the ballet, and she knew she had earned her pride back, but no longer unfettered; it was tempered by nerves – she had felt almost sick before she went on – Or just plain fear, thought Pippa. 'Fear is often the beginning of wisdom,' Angharad would have told her.

After the first curtain call there was, too, an experience for her of which she had often dreamed but had thought probably years ahead: a curtain call of her own – true, only among the lesser parts, and before the principals, but alone. She curtsied – there was quite a roar of applause so that she had to curtsy again. Then, to her astonishment, a footman appeared all in livery, and handed her flowers, not a bouquet wrapped in cellophane but an adorable posy.

From the first minute on the stage she had seen the dell'Orlandos in a box towards the centre of the first tier. Now they were standing up and clapping. The flowers must surely be from them, she thought, and curtsied for the third time, looking directly at them, then, realizing she was holding up proceedings, went to stand beside Humphrey in his Spalanzani costume and who had preceded her; it was next to him and in the front row, that she came forward with the others, again and again.

'There was nothing wrong with the audience tonight,' said Humphrey satisfied.

Pippa, though, was the only one who had flowers.

'They ought to have been for Faye or Maria or Isabelle.'

'Nonsense,' said Humphrey. 'It was a début for you, if only a little one. Besides they don't know anyone in Venice.'

'But it seems you do,' Angharad said. 'I'm dying of curiosity. Who were they from?'

Pippa held out the card. 'Marchese and Marchesa dell' Orlando.'

'The old gentleman in the first-tier box? I noticed them. His wife – I suppose she was his wife – is beautiful,' said Humphrey.

'And you know them?' Angharad was incredulous. 'As far as I know, you and your mother have never been to Italy. Then how?'

Pippa was not going to tell. This was her secret, part of her secret city and, 'I'm as surprised as you are,' she told Angharad – surprised, happy and delighted, which was true. 'They must have been in the audience.' True, too, and it rang true. Angharad was satisfied and not only with this.

'Pippa was really good,' she told Pem. 'To anyone who knows.'

★

97

Later, Angharad, going down to give letters to the stage doorkeeper for posting, stepped outside to the little courtyard for a breath of air. In a few minutes she had a meeting with Humphrey. The first person she saw was the gondolier she had come to recognize, standing with Juliet.

He had drawn her there after he had stopped her as she came with the other girls on their way to Nino's. 'Signorina Juliet. Excuse me, but is Pippa not with you?'

'I wouldn't tell you if she were,' said Juliet.

'That is not friendly. You were nice to me yesterday.'

'I didn't know who you were.'

'Ah, a gondolier? And what, Signorina, is wrong with that?'

'Nothing, only I don't think you are a suitable friend for Pippa.'

'How strange! My mother does not think she is a suitable friend for me. Gondoliers have mothers, Signorina,' and Juliet had to laugh. If I were Pippa, she thought, I couldn't help myself.

Angharad was too far off to hear them but she saw Juliet pat his arm. 'Pippa'll be coming down soon.' She gave him a quick kiss and ran after the others.

'Pippa, you really must go home now,' said Angharad.

I can't, thought Pippa, I could dance all night.

'Get some sleep.'

'I'll never sleep.'

'Pearl and Constance haven't gone yet, go with them,' but Pippa dallied. She took off the white dress and when it was on its hanger in the rack of costumes, covered it carefully with a sheet as Bertha had instructed, then slowly put on her jeans and shirt.

'Are you coming?' called Pearl.

'You go. I'll catch up with you,' but she sat down to

take off her makeup. The music of her solo was still in her head; she did a few steps, then, 'Idiot,' she told herself, picked up her posy and bag, snapped off the lights and ran down the stairs, past the stage door and full tilt into Nicolò who had come from the courtyard to wait there.

'*Mamma mia!* I thought you were never coming.' He sounded put out. He's terribly spoiled, thought Pippa, but he explained, 'They are dining out. The gondola will not be needed for two hours. Already we have wasted half an hour.' His crossness vanished. 'Pippa, *mia*. I want to take you home.'

'In the gondola? Oh, Nicolò.'

'Say Nico.'

'Nico, that would be perfect, a perfect end to a perfect evening. Look, Nico, they gave me flowers.'

'I know. I had to fetch them from the florist. Come.'

'I must write and say thank you. You must give me their proper address. I'd better write it down.'

'Not now. I did not come only to take you home. I want to talk to you. I *need* to talk to you.'

'What about?' But he had handed her into the gondola, and pushed off with a vigorous push. '*Ohé*,' he called as they shot along the narrow canal but he did not turn in the direction of the Pensione Benvenuto; they crossed the Grand Canal into the labyrinth of smaller ones until he ran the gondola beside the steps of a small square, a *campiello* where there was a church that seemed familiar.

'Isn't that San Giuseppe?'

'Yes. My mother always says I should ask San Giuseppe for success in what I do but I get along very well without San Giuseppe.'

'Then why have you brought me here?'

'Because it is very important.' Nicolò had no idea he had contradicted himself.

The little church, its bands of white marble gleaming in the moonlight, was shuttered and quiet; the moon,

fuller now, showed the *campiello* empty, the only movement was the filigree shadow on its flagstones as the
solitary tree stirred its branches – a balmy breeze had
sprung up. The water in the canal shone silver.

Nicolò made the gondola fast and, instead of helping
Pippa out, to her surprise got into it and knelt in front of
her. 'They gave you flowers . . .' he began.

'Yes, but I was the only one who had them. They
should have gone to a principal.' Then she asked, 'Nico,
were you there?'

'Yes. They let me in to stand at the back. Everyone
knows Nico,' he boasted.

'And did you like it?'

'The barcarolle and, yes, the act with – how do you
say it? – the harlot, but the rest,' he shrugged. '*Era noioso*
– it was boring.'

'*Boring!*' Pippa was shocked.

'Oh, it was very clever. How you stay on the tips of
your toes I don't know. I liked some of the men's dancing
– I should like to learn to do that – but most of it was silly
and it went on and on. You were very pretty but you
looked like a girl in a picture. I would put you', and
Nicolò seemed to be seeing a vision, 'in a little black dress,
a skirt up to here,' he showed his thighs. 'The bodice off
the shoulder and low like this,' he put his hand half-way
on her breast, 'black covered in – what do you call these
little things that glitter?'

'Sequins.'

'Yes. Big earrings, black gloves right up the arms,
black leggings —'

'Tights.'

'Yes. Shoes with heels covered in spangles, high, high
heels.'

'High heels are difficult for a dancer.'

'You would not be dancing.' Nicolò was decisive.
'But I did not bring you here to talk about dresses. They

gave you flowers,' he said again. 'I have something else,' and he drew a small packet from his pocket. 'For you. Open it.'

It was wrapped in a shop paper of green patterned with gold. She tore it off; inside was a square green velvet case. Pippa began to tremble. 'No, Nico. No.'

'Yes. Open it.'

She pressed the spring and there, in the moonlight, was the moonstone pendant, shimmering.

'*Nico!*' She pored over it, lifting it out of its case so that it swung on its fine chain catching more light. 'Oh!' Then sense came back. 'But you mustn't.'

'Why not? You wanted it,' he said, as if that explained everything.

'Yes, but I never thought I could *have* it. I couldn't possibly take it.'

His answer was to take the pendant out of her hand, undo the clasp, put it round her neck and fasten it. '*Pietra di luna,*' he said.

But all Cynthia's teaching came back. 'We must never accept expensive presents,' and, 'It's far too expensive.' Pippa said it faintly.

'That is not the way to treat a gift,' Nicolò rebuked her. 'I have plenty of money if that is what is worrying you. Though I was saving to get my own gondola I can get a gondola anytime. Not this.'

'Not this,' Pippa echoed and watched the moonstone's lustre. When she held it there was a jewel coolness but it warmed under her hand.

'Signorina Pippa! To talk about money with a beautiful thing is to make it cheap.'

The word cheap hurt and she cried, 'I didn't mean that but, Nico, such a present!'

'Ah!' and he laughed. 'It is not a present. It has a price!'

'A price! What price?' For a moment Pippa was half afraid: was this what people warned you about? 'They think you can be bought' – she could imagine Angharad saying it but Nicolò dispelled that at once.

'You have to earn it.'

'How could I?'

'First, you must come to my mother's house tomorrow afternoon.'

'Tomorrow. It's Saturday. We have a matinée at five.'

'Then early, two o'clock in the afternoon. She invites you.'

That was true. 'If you take this girl to the Marchesa's, why not here?' Leda had demanded.

'Mamma. You said —'

'You should have used your sense. If Signora Marchesa permits her, why not I?'

'Signorina Pippa, in my mother's house, I will show you what we are talking of,' and Nicolò said impressively, 'I once told you I have a band. It is professional, highly professional, five men. Two of us play the guitar – I am the best. Gianni, second guitar and accordion – he you have met, he was with me at Carlo's. Luigi – we call him Gigi – is drummer, Piero saxophone, violin, anything, even harmonica. Alfio, he has the keyboard. He will show you. It, itself, could almost be the band. We are – what you say? – pop, rock, blues, rap. I, yes, I write the songs. We are not well known yet. We play cafés, disco, here and on the islands, but now we have a try-out for three nights at the Hotel Imperiale at the Lido in their Rotonda. We have never been asked to the Lido before, the Imperiale is deluxe, most deluxe of all so for us it is moment-ous' – Nicolò split the word to make it more important. 'Rich, rich people stay there. It could be the future of our band, and so we need something special. You.' Nicolò said it with his irresistible smile.

'But, Nico, how could I dance with a pop group? I wouldn't know how.'

'Not dance, sing like I heard you in Carlo's and tonight

you sang that aria in the ballet, you, not that doll person. I recognized your voice because I know about voices.' He said it with certainty. 'Yours can reach a theatre up to the balcony. You would find the Rotonda easy. True, you would have to move your hips, sway, rock a little – I will teach you. For the Lido we shall not only do rock, à la mode songs, from London, Naples, America, we shall do Venetian as well. We do not start until next Thursday so there will be plenty of time to rehearse. You will rehearse in the afternoon at my house. I will fetch and take you back. Mamma has a friend who will make your dress — '

'Nico, don't go so fast. *Think!* How can I do two things at once? Our ballets and your band at the Lido.'

'I have thought. We do not begin our show until ten. You finish at the *teatro* by half past ten. If you appear for us at eleven or half past that will be fine. Gianni will fetch you from La Fenice by canal – he has a water-taxi very fast. He will take you back after your act to the *pensione*. You should be in bed by one o'clock, plenty of sleep. You see, I have thought of *everything*,' said triumphant Nicolò, '*and* I shall not pay you but you will keep the *pietra di luna*. Business transaction.'

'Business transaction.' Some of the shimmer seemed to have gone from the moonstone. 'How shall I arrange it with the other girls?'

'Juliet will help you. She is what you call "sport". After the flowers they know you have friends.' He came closer. 'Pippa, *amore*, it is only three nights,' and he said, with Nicolò wiliness, 'We should have such fun.'

'It would be fun,' said Pippa.

X

'Mamma, this is Pippa. Pippa, this is my mother, Leda.'
Nicolò was proud on both counts.

'*Buona sera*, Signora.' Pippa saw a big woman, tall as
Nicolò and as handsome, her hair in a heavy coil on her
neck; her skin was as smooth as his, almost rosy – Don't
they say if you have a lot of olive oil your skin does look
like that? thought Pippa. Her dark eyes, Pippa was sure,
could be fierce, now they were full of curiosity. Her laugh
as she joked with Nicolò was rollicking but Pippa knew
she was taking in every inch of her, in protection of
Nicolò. Then the look softened as, 'You never told me,'
she said to him as the Marchesa had said, 'she is so pretty.'

'*È bellissima*. She is beautiful,' he corrected her.

They had climbed the four flights of stairs so steep and
narrow that there was a rope on brass rings along the wall
to hold on to. 'You will think we live in the sky,' said
Nicolò, and in the narrow hall Pippa looked out on the
rooftops, chimney pots, television aerials, before Nicolò
hustled her in.

The kitchen was welcoming: the big cooking stove
was lit, the rack over it empty as the clothes had been
bundled out of sight. The pans and china on the dresser
had been washed, polished, and shone; the geraniums
were freshly watered and Pippa liked the strings of garlic
and onions, the bunches of dried herbs hanging from the
beams. Even Leda's work-basket had been tidied. The
bright oilcloth on the table had been covered with a lace
cloth and spread. 'Mamma, she will just have had coffee
and a *panino*. They always do after rehearsal.'

'*Gli Inglesi bevono sempre il tè,*' Leda had insisted. 'The English always drink tea. Besides, no guests come to my house without hospitality.'

'She is not a guest. She comes to work. Mamma, there is not time. She has to go at half past three – it is a matinée day so there is a performance at five, another at eight. The Company has been let off early which is why Pippa is able to come. Already it is past one o'clock!' Nicolò said in despair, but the table had tea-glasses ready in their holders, with sliced lemon and sugar, and there were biscuits, a plum cake and an apple tart on Leda's best plates with lacy paper doilies.

'Tomorrow I shall take her straight to the best room.'

'Tomorrow is tomorrow. This is today.'

'We have to be quick,' Nicolò said as they sat down.

'But your mother has made such a wonderful feast.'

'We must be quick.' He was inexorable, and, All you think about, thought Pippa, is your damn band. The moonstone on its chain was under her shirt, close to her heart, and that was her trouble: when he gave it to me I thought for a moment he was fond of me, silly fool me! Business transaction! I should have thrown it back at him but I wasn't going to let him see I cared, and when Leda coaxed, '*Ancora un po*'?' Pippa defiantly took another large slice of plum cake.

The band came and were introduced. 'Gianni, you know him already, Luigi – Gigi – Piero, Alfio,' all young and in their way almost as handsome as Nicolò. Gianni, thick-set and swarthy. Gigi, a slip of a man with a beard, whose hair was auburn red, his eyes blue-grey. Alfio; Piero, whose eyes grew wistful as they looked at Pippa. They eschewed the tea but fell upon the food, eating as they stood round while Nicolò told how he and Gianni had heard Pippa sing at Carlo's – Gianni blew a kiss in the air – and in the *teatro*. The exuberance was infectious and Pippa laughed as she said, 'Wait till you hear me sing before you believe Nico and Gianni.'

The food was finished – there was no more left – and, 'Are we *never* going to begin?' asked Nicolò.

Pippa was given no time really to take in this 'best room', and had only an impression of redness from curtains, sofa and armchairs, the patterned carpet, of many photographs and ornaments, the plastic carnations, which she thought for an instant were real then realized they were too lavish. She did pause a moment to look at the picture of Christ with his Sacred Heart exposed on his red robe, gold rays coming from it, and wondered what it meant until Nicolò commanded her, 'Come and stand by me,' and they began.

The noise was deafening in that small room, made louder when Nicolò sang into the microphone; he was in the centre with his guitar, his whole body rocking to the rhythm. No one, for a moment, was still. Gianni went from his guitar to the accordion while Piero changed from his saxophone, which wove in and out of the melody, to the trumpet when he almost blew out the window. Luigi-Gigi was in ecstasy with his drums, Alfio's hands like lightning on the keyboard, its presses and buttons. 'Do you see?' said Nicolò, when the song finished. 'Not only hear but see?'

'I see.' Pippa was beginning to understand the fascination of the band – professional herself, she recognized its professionalism, also that it was not only a band, it was a brotherhood.

'We call ourselves "I Bolidi". That means The Meteors. What you say fireballs that travel very fast and have great sparkle, energy and light.'

'I Bolidi. What a perfect name,' said Pippa. Sparkle,

energy, light. And they're letting me in! It was a warming thought.

She had exclaimed at the beauty of their instruments. Nicolò had two guitars, one the conventional guitar he used when he played as he moved about in restaurants and sometimes, though rarely, when he played in a concert at the Conservatorio. He let Pippa take it. 'It's lovely to hold!' Beautifully balanced, its sides and back were of fine mahogany, the front of golden yellow spruce, the fingerboard rosewood with nylon strings for a deeper mellow tone. His second guitar was electric, smaller, of wood again, 'Always wood for music,' said Nicolò, but veneered with plastic, glossily black and red. It had, to Pippa, a strange look with two cut-out neck shapes below the fingerboard. 'It exactly fits my body,' he explained. The fingerboard was rosewood again, the frets silverplated, the strings steel to give a brilliant sound.

Gianni's electric guitar was the same; Pippa had already seen his big accordion, once more of wood, plastic-coated and inlaid with brilliant small flowers.

Piero let her try his saxophone, and his shining brass trumpet. She exclaimed at the size of his harmonica, silver inlaid, like Gianni's accordion, with the same metallic flowers.

Luigi-Gigi proudly showed her his set of drums – they all wanted to show off their treasured instruments. He had five drums, again wood, plastic-finished in black with silver rims and struts; the largest, standing on the floor, he worked with his foot on a single big drumstick. His hand drumsticks were hickory wood, his brushes of steel which opened like small fans and he had two brass cymbals standing tall, one single, one double. 'They are really for elegance,' Nicolò told her. 'Alfio can do cymbals on his keyboard.'

The keyboard was, to Pippa, who had only seen small

ones at school, the most fascinating of all: an ordinary keyboard of black and white notes, but big, standing on slim iron legs, it was set in a panel of finger presses and a long line of buttons. ' "Touch response",' quoted Alfio, which meant they only had to be touched to get a multitude of sounds; underlying rhythms and accompaniments, voices, cymbals, tremolos, bells. 'Alfio can extemporize as we go along.'

Alfio wanted Pippa to try it but Nicolò was growing restless. '*Basta*,' he told Alfio, 'Pippa, we'll do "Santa Lucia" to warm you up and let you get the feel of the band. Then, will you let them hear you sing Maria's song "I'm pretty"? You know it so well and it will be one of your songs at the Lido. Try.' Pippa tried, it came out well and they applauded. Well, they would, thought Pippa. She was still uncertain.

'Now, let us see if you can sing this.' He gave her two sheets of music. 'First read it with me.' Their heads close together, she read while he sang the words softly into her ear. 'Now, try with me quietly.' They tried while the band waited, respectfully silent. 'Again.' They sang it again. 'Now, see if you can sing it out with us,' and to the band, 'Not too loud and not fast.'

Pippa stumbled through the Italian words. 'Never mind the accent, just sing.' Then, 'Again.' This time it was quicker. 'Now stand away. Sing it out.' He was suddenly the commander again, sure and firm with them all. The rhythm of the music thrilled through Pippa and she began to feel its potency. Completely supple – 'After all, I am a dancer' – she found her hips moved instinctively, feet, hands and head and, when the song was over, the band really clapped. '*Brava*,' cried Nicolò. He was out of breath, she, long trained, was not. 'If you begin like this it will be very good,' and he asked Pippa, 'Isn't it fun?'

'*Molto* fun!' and, Oh! I'm going to like this, she thought.

Then Angharad threw a cog in the wheels. Such a cog, 'That it makes it impossible,' said Pippa.

In the dressing room, before she could even make up for the matinée, Angharad sent for her. 'I have to talk to you – seriously.'

Could she have found out about the band? Pippa was startled but, Angharad began, 'Pippa, I'm still not easy about you being so much with Juliet.'

'Juliet? But I've told you, Angharad, she's my dearest friend.'

'I know, that's why I'm uneasy. You share a room, don't you? I don't think your mother would like it.'

'*Cynthia?* Why ever not?'

'Pippa, Juliet's a talented dancer but all the same she's common and she's a tart.'

'She's *not*,' flamed Pippa. 'She's just friendly.'

'Friendly! I know Juliet better than you do, Pippa, and now I've seen it with my own eyes. She's going about with a gondolier. A gondolier! Imagine it.'

That's not Juliet, that's me. But Pippa could not say it, not yet. She put her hand up and felt the moonstone; there was too much to jeopardize.

Angharad was going on. 'With Juliet that means it will end in an affair. I am sure your mother wouldn't like it and, as the Company is responsible for all of you, Humphrey agrees.'

'Humphrey does?' It was getting more and more ominous.

'Yes. So after the performance tonight I shall come back to the *pensione* with you and you will pack. We think it best that you come and stay with me at my apartment.'

Angharad had had a battle with herself, a battle she knew she wanted to lose. 'Don't do it,' an inner voice told her. 'Angharad, you're in danger. Don't do it again. You think you have a reason but is it a genuine one? You know it isn't. Don't do it again.'

'But Pippa's so young, and she likes me . . . more than likes, she loves me. She has *shown* it.' Angharad threw that defiantly at her more sensible self.

At the end of last night Pippa, flushed and triumphant, had come off stage and straight to Angharad standing in the wings. 'I've often thought what it would be like to have my own curtain call. Now I *know*! And it's all owing to you.'

She had thrown her arms round Angharad, hugged and kissed her, and now Angharad heard herself saying, 'It's a beautiful apartment, Pippa. Though it's modern it's real Italy, not like the *pensione*. We should have such fun. I'll take you to Carlo's.'

But Pippa was older than she had been a week ago. 'It's very kind, Angharad, but I can't.'

'Why not?'

'I should never live it down with the other girls.' Pippa was blunt. 'Already they call me Anghie's pet.'

'Does that matter so terribly?' Angharad sounded wistful. 'Surely the other girls don't matter now.'

'They do, enormously to me. I have to work with them, you see, be with them,' and she said desperately, 'Juliet's not having an affair. If she were I would know.'

'You're so innocent.'

'You mean stupid. Well, I'm not. If I'm old enough to be in the Company, I'm old enough to look after myself.' She never imagined herself speaking to Angharad like this and stopped, dismayed. 'I'm sorry if I'm ungrateful but please, Angharad, leave me where I am.'

'I'm afraid it's decided.' Angharad was cold. 'The Skinners have been told. We telephoned your mother and she approves.'

'Telephoned Cynthia! Without asking me!'

'There was no need. Some things have to be decided
for you, as you very well know. I'll take you now – I have
a water-taxi – to the *pensione* and you will pack. I'm sorry
if it's distasteful to you but you will come and stay with
me.' She did not say 'under my eye', but it was implied.
Then she softened. 'It isn't a *palazzo* but it's a lovely flat.
You'll see, Pippa,' and she appealed, 'As this has to
happen, let's enjoy it. I know I shall.' She tried to speak
lightly. 'Have you ever thought it's quite lonely being
me?' There was a deeper plea in that but Pippa did not
hear it.

The water-taxi went down one canal after the other, the
houses each side throwing reflections from their lit windows so that the water was stippled with light, the lamp-
posts on the bridges and along the *fondamente* shone. The
taxi went so fast that Pippa could not really see until, I'm
sure I know this canal, she thought. I'm sure that's the
dell'Orlando *palazzetto*. She did not say it aloud and next
minute the water-taxi turned and stopped at a large white
house with balconies on every floor, facing a wider stretch
of water, with lights on the far side; the steps of the house
were new and had scrolled-iron rails, ferns and flowers in
pots. 'Here we are,' said Angharad.

'You see, it's not too bad.' The apartment was cool
and spacious; in the daytime it was shaded by long brown
blinds like awnings that shaded the balcony too. Though
it was modern, the floors were marble but everything in
its spaciousness was plain, with plain white silky matting
on the marble, the furniture sparse, each piece seeming to
complement the others. There were abstract paintings on
the white walls. The simplicity was strangely soothing
after all the ornateness and grandeur Pippa had seen. 'If I
had a home in Venice it would be like this,' said Angharad,

and Pippa, as her jangled nerves began to relax, thought she agreed.

It had been a painful leaving. The water-taxi had waited outside the *pensione* while Angharad came wth Pippa to her room and stayed while she packed. No girls were about: most had gone to Nino's, the rest were having the *pensione* supper. 'We have to save our money. Everything's so expensive here,' but Juliet came in.

'What the . . . What?' Then she stood still. 'I see.'

'What do you see?' Angharad said blandly. 'Pippa is coming to stay with me.'

'How nice for you.' Juliet's eyes blazed and, to Pippa, 'I hope it will be as "nice"', she mimicked the word, 'for you.'

'Come, Pippa.'

'Goodnight,' said Juliet as Pippa, in hopelessness, picked up her case. 'Goodbye.'

On the way down the steps she had given a sad farewell pat to the lions but now, in the apartment, Angharad could not have been more kind. She showed Pippa her bedroom, which matched the sitting room in simplicity, its furniture white too, though the walls were pale blue, and a vase of little roses was on a table by the wide bed; the reading light – its shade matching the cream matting on the floor – was lit, welcoming. 'More comfortable than the *pensione*, I hope,' said Angharad. 'Let's have some supper.'

Pippa had to admit it was very comfortable: a small table was laid for two, set out with a carafe of wine; on a hot-plate trolley was a dish of *fettuccine*, deliciously cooked, and then stuffed aubergines. 'Caterina, the maid, leaves it for me before she goes to bed.' All at once, in spite of Leda's tea, Pippa was hungry. They finished with strawberries and cream. Angharad treated her absolutely as an equal, filling her glass and talking, not of dancing – 'We've had enough for one day' – but of other visits she had made to Italy, to Rome and Venice, Verona, Milan, 'which you'll see.'

As suddenly as Pippa had been hungry, she was tired. It had been a long day, two performances and the band. It's a miracle I got through. Had not Angharad said, 'You did very well tonight'? Satisfied and at peace – Almost, thought Pippa: she did not like remembering Juliet and there was the band. What am I going to do about the band? But she was too tired to think of that tonight and she gave a large yawn.

'I'm keeping you up,' said Angharad and, as they stood up, 'Shouldn't I help you clear up?' asked Pippa.

'Caterina will do that,' and, 'Tomorrow's Sunday. No need to hurry in the morning. Go and have a good night's sleep,' Angharad had herself well in hand but two words slipped out, 'my darling.'

Pippa was too sleepy to hear.

XI

'I am tied up all day,' Angharad told Pippa at breakfast.
'I'll be flying with Humphrey to Verona to see that
everything there is arranged but you'll be going with the
others to Murano, won't you?'

'Murano?'

'The island where they blow the glass. Venetian glass
is famous, though I think it's hideous. Didn't you know,
Pippa, that an excursion has been arranged for the Company to see Murano, some of the other islands and go to
the Lido for lunch and the afternoon?'

'I did know,' said Pippa, 'but I forgot. In any case I
won't be going.'

'Oh!'

'I'm spending the day with . . . with friends.'

'What friends?'

'They sent me the bouquet, remember?'

Last night, as Angharad was hustling her out of the
theatre, the stage doorkeeper had given Pippa a letter.
There had been no time to read it then, nor when they
came back, and it was not until bedtime that she was able
to open it:

Dear Pippa
I see by the papers you have no performances
tomorrow, Sunday. If so, it seems a pity that, on this
your first visit, you have not seen more of our city and
its treasures. Would you like to? If so, unless I hear to
the contrary, Nicolò and I will pick you up at ten
thirty.

Pippa held it out now to Angharad.

'Who is Nicolò?'

'Their gondolier. They have their own gondola.'

'How do you know?'

'I went to tea with them.'

'You never told me.'

'No.'

Angharad read on:

Afterwards we shall go to a restaurant La Locanda on Torcello, one of the islands. I hope you will find it even better than Carlo's.

'How does she know you've been to Carlo's?'

'I told her.'

Eduardo will join us.

'Who is Eduardo?' The inquisition went on.

'The Marchese.'

And Pax Pemberton. A domani.

Angharad handed back the crested letter. 'You do seem to move in exalted circles.'

'Yes.' Pippa would have had to confess she felt gratified and, 'May I phone her? She doesn't know I've left the *pensione*.'

She spoke to Giacomo and, when she had given him the message, added, 'Would you tell Signora Marchesa that I promised Nicolò I would be ready to rehearse with him at half past three?' But what, thought Pippa, was the use of rehearsing with the band now? She knew she could not evade Angharad, especially when it would mean coming home at one o'clock or thereabouts in the morning; Angharad would stop it at once. It was a mercy that

she had leapt to a conclusion with Juliet and Nicolò. Poor
Juliet! thought Pippa. I ought to have made Angharad
understand it was me, not Juliet, but if I had . . . Imagine
the rumpus and – I have to keep this hidden, she decided.
It was strange how that need seemed to go on though, 'It
can't happen now,' she told herself. Then again, It will be
molto fun, exactly as if it were going to happen and,
without saying anything further, she let Angharad go.

The flat was empty. Caterina had already gone for her
twenty-four hours at home. Outside, bells were ringing.
People would be going to church; she went to the balcony
and a cacophony of bells, voices, splashings burst on her.
The wide stretch of water was full of boats, sailing-boats
among them. All along the houses on the bank, shutters
were clacking as they were flung back. Women were up
in the *altane*, those railed wooden roof-houses; they called
to one another. Somewhere near, children were playing –
she could hear their shrill voices and shouts.

The sky was a serene blue, everything shone. The
water was sparkling; the vegetable barge she had seen
before came slowly along, stopping every hundred yards
or so. A smart motorboat swept by with a blue and white
canopy; far away she could hear a gondolier's whistle and
cry, '*Ohé*' – perhaps it was Nicolò coming to fetch her.
She must hurry to put on her strawberry pink dress. The
dilemma about the band seemed to fade. 'You don't know
what will happen,' a voice seemed to tell her. 'Go out and
enjoy yourself. Leave this for now.'

'Why! You are only just round the corner from us,' said
the Marchesa. 'Our *palazzetto* is on the next canal to this.
We could have walked,' and as Nicolò turned the gondola,
'I thought we would keep away from San Marco and the

piazza, they are so crowded on Sundays, and Nicolò tells me you go there most days, so we will take you to the Frari, our Franciscan church, fourteenth-century, Pippa, Santa Maria Gloriosa dei Frari.'

'I have brought you here for two reasons,' said the Marchesa as they stood in the big church with its stretches of marble floor and its almost overpowering mammoth tombs. 'One reason is to see two paintings, my favourites, the angels in Bellini's triptych which is in the Lady Chapel, and this Titian.'

Pippa had seen it as soon as they had come in: over the high altar it dominated the church and she stood gazing at the magnificent picture.

'Do you see,' said the Marchesa, 'how the red of her robe is echoed by the red of the tunic one of the supplicants left on earth is wearing as he cries to her?'

'And people still cry to her?' Pippa knew the answer to that from the Basilica and its candles, the humble little Madonna by the bridge and her fresh flowers.

'Of course. She is our go-between, which is why she is so popular.'

'But is she real to you?'

'She is real. Christ had a mother,' and the Marchesa teased, 'There is even a family tree for her done in mosaic in the Basilica, though that is legendary, but it's almost time for my other reason for coming here this morning.'

Pippa had been half aware of noise and movement but now she heard a gale of laughter and high voices. A troop of little boys and girls were sliding and slithering on the polished marble floor, the boys, obviously in their best, had each a wide white ribbon tied in a bow on his arm; the girls were in long white dresses, all alike, white shoes

and wreaths of white roses on their hair. All were shriek-
ing in excitement. 'But this is a *church*,' said Pippa
shocked.

'I don't think Our Lord would object to a little gaiety,'
and the Marchesa picked up a little girl who had fallen
bump on her bottom at their feet, talking to her in Italian
while smoothing and rearranging her dress and straight-
ening the wreath. 'This is Serafina Pensaro. She and the
other children are making their first communion. They'll
be solemn enough in a moment. Serafina, say good
morning to the signorina.'

'*Buon giorno*,' whispered Serafina, suddenly shy.

'That's a pretty dress you have on,' Pippa said to her,
and when the Marchesa translated the small face lit up.

'They used to have wonderful dresses that had been in
the families for years, fine muslin tucked and frilled and
embroidered, but they led to such envy and, for the
poorer people, a feeling of being inferior, that the Church
laid down that all dresses were to be the same, like a
miniature habit for a nun but in white. They still, though,
get handed round – last Sunday another little cousin wore
this dress, today is Serafina's day. I am her godmother.'

'That must be very special.' Pippa did not think she
had a godmother.

'Yes. Would you believe it?' said the Marchesa. 'I have
thirty godsons and -daughters from different families.
Eduardo has more but we like it and it means being closer
to our people on the estate. But I must hush. It's time to
begin.'

A young monk had come in to light the candles on the
altar; mothers, fathers, grandparents, elder brothers and
sisters captured the children, hastily tidying them up. A
priest in vestments came to fetch them, while whole
families and their friends were assembling, everyone from
great-grandparents, great-uncles and -aunts down to tod-
dlers and babies all elegantly dressed, visiting one another

in their pews, chattering and laughing. Many carried presents, gift-wrapped.

Near where the Marchesa and Pippa were sitting was a table with a fine white cloth, silver vessels and candles and, symbolically, sheaves of wheat and grapes in a crystal bowl.

Then, when the organ began, everyone was still and, in a moment, stood up, as into the church and down the aisle came a procession, led by a boy in cassock and surplice, carrying a tall gold cross. After him came choristers, boys and men, then two priests in gold and white vestments and finally a tall man, vested too with a pointed gold mitre and carrying a crook as if he were shepherding the children, which he was as they walked each side of him, each carrying a flower.

'That's our archbishop,' said the Marchesa. Pippa had never seen a bishop, let alone an archbishop; he looked most imposing. 'A brilliant man. They say he will be the next Patriarch of Venice.'

'An archbishop for children!' said Pippa. 'Is this so important?'

'It is vitally important.' The Marchesa did not whisper but spoke in a low clear voice. 'It is the day on which a child begins to know that what Our Lord Jesus Christ said is true.'

The children came to the altar, genuflected and laid their flowers on it, then separated to go to their chairs set in a semi-circle round the altar, facing the congregation. Their white dresses and bows, the wreaths of white roses on well-brushed hair, shone in the candlelight as the Archbishop yielded his crook and mitre to the priests, all in a tumult of music.

The Mass was in Italian so that Pippa could not understand a word, either of the Archbishop or of the responses or when a boy and a girl read from a lectern, but she and Cynthia had seen a Passion play and she understood when the wheat and grapes, bread and wine were brought by four children from the table to the altar and when, first, the paten with the bread was raised, then the chalice with the wine, both to the accompaniment of the Frari's deep-toned bell. The words in the Archbishop's strong voice rang out. 'This is my body.' 'This is the cup of my blood.' She saw the small heads raised to look, then sink back into folded hands.

The children came one by one to the Archbishop to kneel and be given the Host. The congregation followed, including the Marchesa, while Pippa knelt alone. Then with the Archbishop's blessing it was over, the procession formed and went out. The last view was of mitre and crook high above the children.

In a few moments they came rushing back to where relations and friends were waiting. There was hugging and kisses, glad voices, laughter and presents.

The Archbishop came in: he had taken off his vestments and was in a black cassock, his bishop's cross on his breast; he had a wide magenta sash and wore his *zucchetto*, a small skull cap such as Pippa had seen Jewish men and boys wear, but his was magenta. 'Marcia!' He went straight to the Marchesa and Pippa was astounded to see, when he held out his hand, how she swiftly knelt and kissed his ring.

'This is Philippa Fane, an English girl.' Pippa was still more astonished to feel impelled to copy the Marchesa, kneel, too, and kiss the ring. Perhaps there was something awkward in the way she did it because he laughed and said in English, 'You have never done that before, have you?' and, seeing her flush, 'There, I am only teasing. Really I am most flattered.'

He was so young for an archbishop, so good-looking that it seemed entirely natural to stand there chatting but the children were clustering round him, vying for attention.

'Well, I must go and congratulate Serafina and her family,' said the Marchesa. 'I have a little brooch for her. Then we'll meet Eduardo and Pem for lunch,' but Pippa lingered.

'Signora Marchesa . . .'

'Say "Marcia" like the Archbishop. It doesn't make me feel so old!'

'Marcia,' and Pippa asked, 'What did Jesus say?'

'My dear! Read your New Testament, especially John,' but Pippa did not have a New Testament.

It was not Nicolò who took them to La Locanda on the island of Torcello. 'It's quite a famous restaurant,' said the Marchesa. They went by water-taxi. 'Nico has to go to Serafina's celebration luncheon but he will come and fetch you,' and, 'That's a very beautiful pendant you are wearing.'

Pippa had proudly worn the moonstone outside her dress. 'Yes, Nicolò gave it to me.' She was glad to be able to tell someone about it – she still felt a little uneasy.

'Nicolò! He must be making money.'

'He says he is. Cynthia, my mother, always told me we mustn't take expensive presents but it's not a present, it's a down payment.' She did not know how else to put it. 'Marcia, he has asked me to sing with his band those three nights at the Lido.'

The Marchesa's reaction was not at all what Pippa had expected: not an instant repression of the idea or the opposite, congratulations. Instead, as if she were protecting Nicolò she asked a direct question: 'Can you sing?'

'Ask Mr Pemberton,' said Pippa.

★

The water-taxi took them swiftly across the lagoon to
Torcello, turning into a muddy canal. 'Most of the canals
here are silted up,' the Marchesa explained. 'Torcello has
an old, proud history. It was an important town but
almost all of it has crumbled and not many people live
here now. There are a few farms and market gardens but
mostly they live by tourists.' There were crowds of them
walking along the footpaths on both banks. 'I expect they
are going to the cathedral, Torcello still has a magnificent
cathedral, but some are locals on a Sunday outing, picnick-
ing or having luncheon at one of the cafés along the way.'
The water-taxi had chugged its way past these, open-air
with flowers and bright awnings. 'Not La Locanda, of
course,' said the Marchesa and, as they came alongside a
large wooden landing stage, 'Here we are.'

It was a happy lunch. 'Better even than Carlo's,' Pippa
said ecstatically. The Marchese and Pem were waiting for
them and they were led to a table on a wide terrace under
a canopy of vines through which the sun filtered. The
tables were spread with pale blue cloths, crystal and silver.
On three sides was a flowering garden with, behind it, a
glimpse of tall buildings showing through trees; the fourth
side was on the water.

The Marchese ordered iced flagons of a local white
wine. Pippa had her first taste of asparagus, fresh, young,
green, with Parmesan. After it, *risotto di pesce* – rice with
fish, 'for which La Locanda is famous,' the Marchese told
her.

'I couldn't possibly eat any dessert,' said Pippa when
the waiters brought second menus.

'Try a sorbet,' said the Marchesa. 'They are light and
refreshing. They do a jasmine one which is delicious.'

'You mean jasmine flowers?'

'Yes.'

At the end they sat over coffee, replete and contented.
'I don't want to move again,' said Pem.

'Which reminds me,' said the Marchesa, 'Pippa told me to ask you: can she really sing?'

'Like a flute. I taught her myself and still do. In fact, I wanted her to give up dancing and study singing.'

'I asked because she has to leave us soon. I promised Nicolò.'

'She must visit the cathedral first,' the Marchese said firmly. 'No one can leave Torcello without seeing the Teoteca Madonna . . . it's only minutes away.'

The old piazza was now only a grassed square where the local women had stalls selling gewgaws – postcards, beads and needlework – and, led by the Marchese, they came into the spaces of the cathedral with its huge mosaics at either end. It was thronged with people but he took Pippa's elbow and steered her away from the giant mosaic of the Crucifixion, the Resurrection and the gruesome Last Judgement to the opposite wall. 'Now look up,' he said, and there she was, against a gold background, quietly dominating the great church. 'The Teoteca Madonna,' the Marchese said.

She was not comely, even plump like the other madonnas Pippa had seen but tall, thin, almost emaciated; she was wrapped in a dark blue mantle and veil, which made her seem an oriental woman. Her eyes looked steadfastly but as if she did not like what she saw. 'If you look more closely you will see tears on the mosaic.' Her right hand pointed towards the haloed golden child she carried. 'The hope of the world,' said the Marchese. 'She is more than eight hundred years old and she has never smiled. I don't think, with the world as it is, she ever will. We must pray, Pippa,' but Pippa suddenly felt she had had a surfeit of madonnas and whispered, as had hundreds of thousands before her, to the glimmering figure and Child above them, 'I'm too busy now. Some other time.'

She walked back from the cathedral to the water-taxi

with Pem. 'Pem, if I tell you something will you promise not to tell anyone else?'

She was so deeply in earnest that he had to smile. 'I can keep secrets as long as it's not anything too bad.'

'It might be good for me, a good experience and it would be fun and I want to do it.'

'That settles it, then.'

'But I'm not sure.'

'Why ask me?' said Pem.

'Because you *know*. Eduardo and Marcia have a private gondola and their own gondolier, Nicolò but that's not all he is . . .' and it came out, Pem standing still as he listened, Pippa's words tumbling over themselves in her eagerness, ending with, 'He has given me this pendant as a down payment.'

'Has he, now?' Then Pem was serious. 'The Company won't like this, Pippa.'

'I know, which is why I don't want them to know. It's nothing to do with them if I do it in my own time,' argued Pippa.

'It would be if you got over-tired.'

'It's only for three days.'

'True.'

'But', said Pippa, 'I don't know anything about bands. You do, and about every kind of music. I've heard you play jazz and pop. We're rehearsing this afternoon at Nicolò's mother's flat. He is coming to fetch me in his friend's water-taxi. Pem, could you – would you come, too, listen to us and tell me if you think it would hurt my voice and if the band's worthwhile – worth fighting for?'

'Will you have to fight?'

'I can guess so.' But Pippa pushed the reminder of Angharad out of her mind. 'Will you, Pem?'

'A busy and eminent man to be bothered with this!' The Marchesa said when he told her. For once she was disapproving. 'What impertinence!'

'Divine impertinence. That's what I call it,' said Pem.
'It's not for herself, it's for the band.'
    'You'll go?'
    'Yes, I'll go.'

'It's a mixture of rock, soul, as they call it, and blues,' said
Pem to Pippa as they left Leda's flat. 'And he has it right.
I particularly liked that almost blues "Sun In My Bones",
beautifully lazy and paced, and the one about "A Bowl of
Stars".'
    'Nicolò wrote them.'
    'Then he's something of a poet as well as a musician. I
like, too, his reviving of the old Venetian songs. Nowadays they are usually imports from Naples or London
and America. The Venetian songs will suit your voice.'
Pippa noticed he said 'will' not 'would'. 'Yes, the young
man has talent.'
    'That's what I thought. You think I should do it?' She
could not have been more eager.
    'I see no harm, but how can you do it, Pippa?' She
had told him she was with Angharad now. 'Angharad
would never countenance it, nor, I think, would
Humphrey.'
    'No,' said Pippa sadly, 'but suppose, if somehow I did
it, would you defend me?'
    'I would.'
    'But how? How can I possibly do it as I'm with
Angharad?'

XII

Angharad was home when Pippa got back.

'Had a good day?'

'What a day!' Pippa was filled to the brim with the day: to be with the Marchesa and Nicolò; the Titian painting; the children and the first communion; La Locanda and the luncheon; the band rehearsal, her own singing and Pem's approval. Now, all at once, she was tired out and longed for bed.

'You must tell me about it. Pippa, I thought we would have a little treat. I'm taking you to dinner at Carlo's.'

'Carlo's!' Pippa could not keep the dismay out of her voice.

'Don't say you don't want to?' Angharad was incredulous. 'I thought you loved Carlo's?'

'I do. I do. It's just that I've been to another marvellous restaurant today called La Locanda on Torcello, and I don't think I could eat two of those sort of meals in one day.'

'Of course you could. The young can always eat, but I see,' said Angharad, 'new friends are better than old.'

'Pem was there,' Pippa retaliated but Angharad did not choose to hear.

'So there's no more use for poor old Angharad.'

'Of course there is. I owe so much to you.'

'Owe! Pippa, I want you to like me for myself.'

'I do. Of course I do. I – I love you.'

But Angharad was not to be placated. 'You don't know anything about love. How it can hurt.'

Angharad was in a strange mood: restless, she walked about picking things up and banging them down; there were red patches on her cheeks and neck. 'Angharad, is there anything wrong?'

'Nothing that matters to you. Only that I've had a hard day. That I'm tired and hungry.'

'Of course it matters.' Pippa found she was saying 'of course, over and over again.

And lonely, thought Angharad, desperately lonely. She had not thought that the closeness of having Pippa in the apartment should be so – dangerous? Pippa had undone her and on the way back from Verona Angharad had made up her mind. The child's so happy with me, she had heard Pippa singing that morning as she dressed, I'll take her to Carlo's, Angharad had planned. We'll have a lovely meal and I'll give her plenty to drink. 'That's not fair,' Angharad's voice told her at once but, 'Only so that she'll be relaxed and it will seem a natural thing.' Angharad had persuaded herself. Now Pippa had upset the apple cart. 'Golden apples,' Angharad mocked bitterly and, 'You'd better go to bed,' she said. 'As you're so tired. It doesn't matter about me.'

'Of course it does' – another of course. 'Give me five minutes to wash and brush and I'll be ready. I'm not nearly as tired as you are. I was just selfish.'

She was so sweetly contrite that Angharad had difficulty in stopping herself taking Pippa in her arms then and there but, 'Not yet,' she told herself sternly. 'Not yet.'

There was more contention at dinner. Angharad was captious, finding fault with the waiters and the food, then gently asking Pippa about her day only to nettle her when she answered.

'I met an archbishop.'

'Dear me! We get grander and grander!'

'He wasn't grand, he was nice,' and when Pippa

described the children and the first communion, 'Catholic treacle. Little girls dressed up like brides. Pah!' said Angharad. 'Pretentious.'

'It wasn't pretentious. It was real.'

'Pippa, that woman is trying to convert you.' Angharad spoke as if it were a virus. 'All Catholics do.'

'She doesn't. I asked questions, and if she did I wouldn't mind.'

'Just because she's a *marchesa*.'

'That isn't fair.'

'I love it when you get angry. You go pink like a rose. I was only teasing.'

But she was not. There was venom, thought Pippa in surprise. Angharad was jealous. *Jealous!* Angharad! And now she was trying to make up.

'Have some more wine.'

Perhaps because she had had wine at lunch too, Pippa began to feel slightly dizzy. 'I don't think I'd better have any more.'

'Nonsense.' Angharad filled her glass. She insisted on giving her brandy as well. Pippa had no idea how she got home.

She was asleep when her door opened and Angharad came in. 'Pippa.'

'Angharad.' Pippa half sat up, rubbing sleep out of her eyes.

Angharad was wearing a white wrapper – it was too silken and flimsy to be called a dressing gown. Her hair was loose, a fall of the flaxen paleness Pippa had admired; now it seemed too heavy and there was a hectic look on her face that startled Pippa wide awake. 'Is there anything the matter?'

'Only what has been the matter for weeks, months,

and you didn't notice.' Angharad laughed but it was a bitter little laugh. 'Were you really blind or did you pretend to be blind like the others?'

'I don't know what you're talking about.'

'Pippa, let me get in with you.'

'Into my bed?' But Angharad was already unfastening her wrapper and Pippa saw with a shock that there was nothing else under it. In a flash she understood. This is what Juliet was trying to warn me about. Had it happened to Juliet too? Pippa tried to be calm. 'I thought you just liked my dancing.'

'Don't talk about dancing. I loved you from the first moment I saw you. You were so sweet and shy. Oh, my darling.' She was in the bed.

Pippa backed to its edge but an arm held her. 'Come closer.' Angharad's other hand was undoing the buttons on her pyjamas – she only slept in the top, without the trousers. 'Your little breasts, like buds.' No one had touched Pippa's breasts before; now Angharad kissed them and Pippa felt a tingling go through her. 'Little thing!' The voice was full of tenderness, not frightening but all the same Pippa had to fight to keep her own voice steady as she tried to say lightly, 'I'm not little and I'm not a thing.' Then more desperately, 'I love you, Angharad, but not like this. You must go now.'

'I can't.'

'If you don't I'll scream so loud Caterina will come in.'

'Caterina's away on Sunday. There's nobody here but you and me. Don't be so hard, Pippa. I've been so lonely, so separate. Please. Just be friendly. Stroke me a little. Let me stroke you.'

The arms drew her in. With a shudder but trying to be normal, Pippa asked, 'Would you like me to massage you? I often do that for Cynthia.'

'To hell with Cynthia.' Angharad lost all control. One

arm held Pippa in a fierce grip – a long white arm like the tentacle of an octopus thought Pippa with a gasp of horror. A hand forced her head back and Angharad was kissing her face, eyes and mouth – she felt Angharad's tongue. Pippa tried to dodge the kisses. 'Go. Go back to your bed.'

'Darling, you can trust me. I'll show you. It's wonderful. You'll love it too. I'll be gentle,' and Pippa felt a finger, exploring her. It was only a finger but her shriek went to the ceiling and she fought Angharad, her knee doubled up, her other leg kicking, fists beating. Angharad only seemed to enjoy it; she gave another laugh. A high one, triumphant, and there was another frenzy of kissing, almost suffocating Pippa. The next moment Angharad was on top of her, full weight, but she had reckoned without Pippa's strong lithe dancer's body. Pippa bit her on the mouth, scratched her face, rolled out from under her and tumbled out of bed. 'Now go!' she panted. 'Get out of my room and don't come near me ever again!'

She pulled her pyjama jacket round her, two of the buttons had gone, went into the bathroom and locked the door.

Clean! I must get clean! She ran hot water into the basin and, shuddering, washed and washed, splashing her body. She had blood on her knuckles and in her nails. Then, cautiously, she opened the door a crack and looked: the room was empty. She came out, dressed hastily in her jeans and a shirt, got out her suitcase from the cupboard and packed pell-mell, but the case was heavy and she left it, only taking her bag and jacket.

The apartment was silent, without lights; moonlight from the three-quarter moon coming through the windows showed her the way. She listened for a moment outside Angharad's door. There was the sound of weeping, a sound that followed her as she opened the apartment door, and was running down the stairs. She had trouble with the main door, frantically finding buttons and pressing them but, at last, she was out on the *fondamenta*, where the light was as bright as day, the water silver. There were no boats, no people. It must be very late, she thought. As if in answer a clock struck two. She could hear her own heart beating, thudding. She had to get away, but where? The *pensione*? She imagined the night porter woken, the girls next morning and Juliet, though Juliet would understand. The Marchesa? She could not possibly disturb the Marchesa at this hour of the night but, on that, a wild hope came. Nicolò. Perhaps by good fortune he was sleeping in the gondola. It was a beautiful warm night and he liked to get out of Leda's flat. The *palazzetto*, Signora Marchesa had said, was just round the corner in the next canal but which side? She must run to the head of the nearest one and look right and left.

She started to run – her running broke the quietness. Would Angharad hear and look out of the window? Pippa ran faster in panic. At the head of the canal she turned left but there was no other canal on that side. She turned and ran right, over a small bridge. In her haste she fell on the bridge steps, sending her bag flying, its contents flung out. She gathered them up, comb, compact, handkerchief, postcards from the afternoon at Torcello, stuffed them all in, stood up and looked from the bridge. Yes! There, halfway down the canal, was the *palazzetto* with the unmistakable gondola tied to its post, its brass sea urchins glinting in the moonlight. She ran again, almost tripping on the *fondamenta*. 'Nicolò! Nico! Nico! Wake up.' She could see him lying on the footboards, wrapped in the rug, his head on the cushions. 'Nico, please wake up. Nico, help me.'

He was up already. Did he think I was a thief?

'Pippa! *Mamma mia*! Mother of God! What are you

doing here?' And as he took in her state, 'What has happened? Pippa *mia!*'

'Nico, help me.' Now she was shivering so violently that all she could say was, 'Angharad, Signora Angharad.'

'The senior lady? She hurt you?'

'No. I hurt her,' and Pippa shuddered more. 'Nico, take me away, far away from everybody. I can't see anyone again ever. I can't. I won't.'

He did not ask any more questions. He picked her up, put her in the gondola, wrapping her in the rug – she was still shivering – and went to his oar. 'I know where,' he said.

Crouched on the cushions, she was hardly conscious of the gondola's passage between the still houses, only that the gliding movement was taking her away. The moon went behind a cloud, the silver vanished, but Nicolò whistled softly, whether to her or to himself she did not know but it was a comforting normality. Then as the gondola stopped, he stopped too, leapt ashore and fastened the rope.

It was the *campiello* of San Giuseppe again, the little square empty as it had been before, the church closed and quiet, the single tree, now that the moon had disappeared, without its filigree shadow. 'No one will find us here.' Reassuring and peaceful, it was her *campiello*. Perhaps San Giuseppe would protect her. The shivering and shudders grew less.

Nicolò came to sit beside her. 'You don't have to tell me,' he said. 'That first night when I took you all from Carlo's along the Grand Canal, I saw the senior lady kiss your hair.'

'Don't. Don't.' Pippa shuddered again.

'You are shivering. Lie down beside me.' '*Scaldati accanto a me* – get warm. In the morning we shall think but not now. You should get a little sleep.' He helped her to lie flat on the footboards, a cushion for her head, spread the rug over her, then came in beside her.

The cloud had passed, the moon shone out and she saw his face as he bent over her, the brilliant brown eyes that were now concerned, the soft mass of his hair, the little gold rings in his ears against the olive skin, paled by the moonlight. 'There, there,' said Nicolò. He seemed all that was safe, protective – even more.

He smelt of the clothes he slept in, a little of sweat, of garlic, down-to-earth ordinary things, not like Angharad's exotic scent, which still seemed to be on Pippa's hands, skin and hair. His arm round her was strong. 'Come close.' He drew her closer as Angharad had, and suddenly it was not only warmth and comfort: for all the outrage, Angharad had woken Pippa: she felt tremors of delight, a tingling, then a gust of feeling that made her cling to him. Why should one person touching you fill you with horror and disgust and another with such longing? 'Nico,' she whispered.

'Pippa *amore*.' It was sleepy.

Amore. Love. Real bodily love. She pressed herself closer against him. 'Nico, love me. I want you to make love to me. Show me. I've never done it before so show me.' She pressed closer but the arm that held her had slackened.

'Nico, *amore*.'

She was rewarded by a healthy snore.

XIII

Pippa was woken by the sound of Nicolò's oar in the water. He was standing on the stern, the gondola was moving. Dizzily she knelt up; her head was throbbing – I suppose it was all the drink I had last night. Last night! For a moment she was back in the trauma but a small breeze was blowing and seemed to take it all away.

It was the earliest of early mornings. The sun had just risen and Venice was a city of light and air, of glittering water, of domes that seemed to rise lightly, finding the sunlight as bubbles find prisms of light in their transparent shells. That was what her grandfather's old book had described and, It's true, thought Pippa again, not only illumined but drenched in light. The dark shadows of the night had gone, there was no darkness now under the bridges. The early morning shone, shimmering like her moonstone but with the colours of a rose opal set clear against the sun.

The deepest shadows had a tone of gold, the highest a light of silver. Pippa looked and looked, herself forgotten, then Nicolò sang a soft 'Ohé' as he avoided the vegetable barge. He had turned into a familiar water-street and, 'Where are you taking me?' she asked.

'To the Signora Marchesa. Where else?' Nicolò was blithely unaware that he had in any way disappointed Pippa. 'It is not thinkable you should go back to the senior lady. Never again. At the *pensione*, Juliet says the girls are not nice to you. Mamma would be delighted but we have no room. So, Signora Marchesa —'

'We can't wake her so early.'

'She is early. I take her each morning at seven to Mass.'

'Every morning?' That seemed excessive. 'For you, yes,' the Marchesa would have said, 'for me, it is natural.' But, 'Every morning?'

'Si.'

'But . . . I can't possibly ask her.'

'You will not have to. You do not know our *gentilissima* Marchesa.'

When the Marchesa saw Pippa, bedraggled, pallid with tiredness and distress she opened her arms, 'What have they done to you?' and for the first time Pippa began to cry in a storm of tears.

The Marchesa motioned Giacomo and Nicolò away. 'Tell me,' she said.

'I'm . . . ashamed.'

'It sometimes helps to tell,' and Pippa told of every shaming moment as the tears streamed again.

When she had finished, 'Poor woman,' said the Marchesa.

'*Poor?* Angharad?'

'Yes, but thank God you ran away.'

'But what am I going to *do*?' Pippa was desperate.

'First you will have a hot bath, then breakfast with coffee so you can gather yourself together, as you must because I think, Pippa, it is very important that you arrive for your class and rehearsal exactly as usual.'

'I can't.'

'Yes, you can – for yourself and for her. The situation is yours. Be polite, no more than polite, to her.'

'To her?' Pippa drew back in horror.

'Yes. Do you know, Pippa, the best thing you said to Miss Fullerton was, "I love you but not like this." Other girls would turn on her, gossip, exaggerate, but you won't. Not a word to anyone, not even to her.'

'I see,' said Pippa slowly. She was beginning to see.

'Yes,' said the Marchesa. 'Be merciful, then you can never go wrong, and meanwhile would you like to stay here with Eduardo and me for the rest of your time in Venice? Would you like to?'

'It would be heaven.'

Pippa was so touched that the tears were coming again and the Marchesa said quickly, 'I think, first we should telephone your mother. We'll need a little authority. Would you like me to speak to her?'

'Would you?' Then Pippa stopped. 'Marcia, you were going to Mass.'

'There are later Masses.'

When it was Pippa's turn to speak, Cynthia was her usual balanced self. 'Pippa, I'm sorry beyond words that this has happened.'

'I don't want to talk about it.'

'You must try and take it sensibly.'

'It didn't happen to you,' Pippa almost shouted down the telephone.

'Well, darling, we'll talk about it when you come home.'

'I won't talk about it, *ever*!'

'All right.' Tactful Cynthia changed the subject. 'This lady, the Marchesa dell'Orlando, sounds a true friend.'

'She is.'

'You're lucky in having her. I'm so glad. You must tell me all about her and you must stay with her, Pippa. That will relieve my mind. I'll write to Humphrey Blair.'

'But, Marcia, how can I go to class and rehearsal? My things are all at Angharad's.'

'Not now. Giacomo has gone to fetch them, not Nicolò, Giacomo has more authority. They'll be here when you've had your bath.'

'Better now?' The Marchesa asked when, half an hour later, Pippa came in bathed and tidy – she had even washed her hair. 'To get that scent off,' she could have said – and shuddered.

'Drink your coffee,' the Marchesa said and then, as if to turn Pippa's thoughts away, 'There is one thing I must insist on, Pippa, if you are to do this double act – dance every performance and afterwards, for three nights sing at the Lido with quite a long journey and be very late for bed. From today, as soon as your morning's ballet work is done, you must come straight back here – we will have some lunch ready – then rest and I hope sleep on your bed. We'll wake you in time for the evening. Nicolò will take you back and forth to La Fenice.'

'But he wants me to rehearse in the afternoons.'

'Let him want. When the time comes — '

'It's tomorrow. There's so little time.'

'Nicolò will sing with you as he takes and fetches you, Gianni, too, when he fetches you for the Lido in his water-taxi – I understand that is the arrangement. I'm sure you are quick and it is all casual compared to your real work. Otherwise you will be too tired to do yourself justice in either role and your Humphrey Blair will have reason to be cross.'

To Miss Fullerton

The Marchesa could not bring herself to write 'Dear Miss Fullerton'. Though she had seemed calm to Pippa she was burning with indignation. 'It was a carefully thought-out plot,' she told the Marchese. 'Inventing that new role – Pippa says she owes that to her – coaching her in it, then making that flimsy excuse to take the girl to stay with her; also she lied about that, Eddy. I thought I should telephone the director, Humphrey Blair. Though Miss Fullerton told Pippa he approved, he knew nothing about her taking Pippa away from the *pensione* to stay with her. He said, "Good God! I would have stopped it at once." Then trying to bribe her with another dinner at Carlo's, giving her all that drink, and a near rape!'

To Angharad she wrote:

Please allow my butler, Giacomo Ruffino, to collect
Philippa Fane's luggage. She will be staying with us for
the remainder of her time in Venice. You know the
reason why. We have telephoned her mother who is
writing to Humphrey Blair.

Angharad had not come to the theatre until almost time for rehearsal; in fact, she met Martha coming out of the studio. 'Martha, was Pippa in class this morning?'

'Of course. Why not?'

'Thank God.' Angharad looked distraught. Then, 'Martha, would you be kind and ask Jasper to start rehearsal for me? Tell him to do the second act of *Hoffman*. It was a little ragged last night. He'll know. I need to see Humphrey.'

'I have to resign, Humphrey, now.'

'You don't surprise me. Oh, Angharad!'

'So Pippa has been talking.'

'Pippa hasn't said a word. It was Juliet.'

As Juliet was arriving for class she had seen Nicolò outside the stage door. 'Nico, what are you doing here?'

'I have just brought Pippa.'

'*Brought* Pippa?'

'Pippa is not staying with the senior lady any more.'

'O-ho!' said Juliet slowly.

'It is o-ho! She ran away to me. She knows sometimes I sleep in the dell'Orlando gondola on warm nights. By good fortune I was there last night. In the morning I took her to the *palazzetto*.'

'Was she very upset?'

'Whew!' Nicolò gave an expressive whistle.

'It's my fault,' said Juliet. 'I tried to warn her but Pippa lives in a little dancing cocoon of her own.'

'Excuse. What is a cocoon?'

'The silk-thread shell that a grub makes for itself to sleep in until it's time for it to turn into a butterfly. I should have awoken her. You see I knew, and I should have been more explicit. Pippa's not a fool, but I was so sorry for Angharad, the senior lady, I promised her not to tell. That was wrong of me and I'm going to tell now.'

'Juliet, I think best not to talk to Pippa about it.'

'Not Pippa. I'm going straight to talk to Mr Blair.'

'Juliet was one of them, wasn't she?' said Humphrey now to Angharad.

Angharad was looking ill, her face lividly pale, her eyes dark-circled. She was even carelessly dressed, but Humphrey had to go on. 'You haven't been exactly nice or fair to Juliet ever since, have you? No wonder she decided to take revenge, and before her there was Anne Wolfe – we lost her. Maybe this was the reason with others. Certainly if it hadn't been for the Marchesa dell' Orlando, Pippa would have left the Company.'

He sighed. 'It's intolerably sad, Angharad, especially as the Company needs you, and I so like working with you. You have done so much for us but this is real damage and you are right to resign. You should not be where you have to work with girls, especially girls like ours who are as uncommon as they are attractive.' He sighed again and got up. 'I think it's better they don't see you like this, for your sake and Pippa's. I'll put you on a plane this afternoon to London or wherever you want to go. I'm truly, truly sorry but enough is enough.'

'I agree,' said Angharad. 'I'll go and pack.'

Pippa was shocked. 'Angharad's *gone*?'

'For good,' said Juliet with relief, but Pippa went to Humphrey.

'It's because of me, isn't it?' she asked.

'It's because of Angharad. It wasn't your fault.'

'Perhaps it was a little. It just didn't cross my mind. I was blind.'

'Kittens are.' Humphrey tried to lighten it.

'I'm not a kitten.' Pippa had always hated that kind of talk. 'You think I don't know about women lovers. Of course I do. I wasn't born yesterday. It's just that with Angharad – and me – it never crossed my mind. I thought it was all my dancing. She was so wonderful and kind.'

'She was wonderful and kind,' said Humphrey. 'Pippa, always remember that. I doubt if you would have been where you are today without her.'

The best thing for Pippa in these days was to be with Nicolò. On the way to and from the theatre they sang the songs that Pippa was to sing at the Imperiale. He was always punctual, waiting for her.

'Talk about being pampered,' said Juliet.

'Marcia's so kind.'

Juliet had come to see her off and, waiting by the

gondola, Nicolò overheard and, as soon as they left: 'Marcia? You call Signora Marchesa Marcia?'

'She told me to.'

'Of course. You are the stylish English ballerina.'

'Don't be silly. I'm a soloist, that's all. You're jealous.'

'Yes, I am. It was I who found you and brought you to the *palazzetto*. You belong to me.'

She was suddenly still.

Only that morning the Marchesa had said to her, 'Pippa, don't let yourself rely too much on Nicolò. He is, as I very well know, most charming but it is an easy charm, easy come, easy go.'

Pippa had taken the message and, remembering the night in the gondola, had flushed. 'That suits me too,' she had said but her inmost heart said, 'Liar! Liar.'

XIV

On Tuesday and Wednesday nights the Marchesa, without objection, let Pippa go after the performances to rehearse with the band. 'There is so much I have to learn – for instance, I've never used a microphone. We must rehearse.'

'Not more than two hours,' stipulated the Marchesa.

On Wednesday afternoon, Leda's friend brought Pippa's dress to the *palazzetto*. 'My goodness!' said the Marchesa when she saw the briefness of its bouffant black lace skirt, the slip of bodice, off the shoulders and cut low, its satin glittering with black sequins. 'That should fetch them.'

'I think it's lovely,' said Pippa. She had long black gloves. 'Nicolò had bought the almost transparent black tights with seams. 'You must get those straight.' The tights were studded with diamanté stars. He and Pippa had stopped at the Piazza San Marco to buy her high-heeled shoes. 'Not too high,' she had begged Nicolò, 'or I'll fall over.'

'You look,' said the Marchesa, 'what they call a million dollars, but you should have plenty of rouge and eye-shadow under those lights.'

'I just won't take off my ballet make-up.'

'Good.' The Marchesa was enjoying this as much as Nicolò and Pippa. 'I wish I could come and watch you.'

'Come,' coaxed Pippa.

'If I did, everyone would at once become formal and

polite. Nico would not let himself go. Nor would the boys. There are times when one has to keep out.'

Staying with the dell'Orlandos was an enchantment. Pippa's bedroom looked out over the garden: she could smell the scent of the profusion of roses on the terrace. She was woken early by the sun – she refused to have her shutters closed – and the first thing she saw in the morning was the cypress with an outline of gold, recalling the golden early morning with Nicolò. She went happily back to sleep until Giacomo woke her again with coffee, hot rolls and delicious black cherry jam brought to her room.

Everything was taken care of. When she came in from morning class and rehearsal, a late lunch was waiting for her. 'Leda will give you something this evening before you work with the band.' The Marchesa sat with her or played the piano, nothing could have been more restful, and when they talked it was as equals . . . the patrician old lady and the young girl.

'It's all so gracious,' Pippa told Juliet.

'Well, naturally. If you have a title, estates, a butler and cook, a few little things like that.'

'I meant caring about living, making room for it, like setting a table for meals and making it look attractive.'

'You don't have to be a *marchesa* for that.'

'No. Anyone can do it, if you take a little extra trouble. I'm going to do it when I get home.'

There was more to it than that; nothing, Pippa sensed, to do with having a title and money: there seemed to be a whole new dimension. Nicolò had told her that the dell'Orlandos had innumerable griefs and worries. Their only son had been killed in a car accident – 'I think that is why they like me so much.' There were many troubles:

land had had to be sold, estate after estate. 'There used to be ten servants here, now there is only Giacomo, a woman to clean and the old cook who must be eighty.' The Marchese, too, had been defeated in politics and yet they both had a serenity untroubled, with a quality of . . . 'joy' was the word that came to Pippa – or was it faith?

On the Tuesday evening, 'Marcia,' she asked, 'are you going to Mass early tomorrow?'

'Yes.'

'Could I come with you?' The Marchesa hesitated and Pippa was quick to say, 'Not if you'd rather not. I might disturb you.'

'Of course you wouldn't. I should love you to come but, my dear, this is Wednesday. You have a matinée, another performance in the evening and this evening you have your last rehearsal with the band. You should stay in bed and get all the sleep you can.'

'I know, but I'm too excited to sleep much.'

The Marchesa still hesitated. 'The Mass can't be understood all at once.'

'I know. You told me to read the New Testament, but I haven't one.'

'Then let yourself feel it, don't worry about exact following. Very well.'

It was a wet dismal morning without a trace of gold. 'I never thought of it raining in Venice,' said Pippa.

'Only too often.'

She had not brought a raincoat. 'I never thought I'd need it.' Anything of the Marchesa's was too long for her so the cook lent her a cloak that came down to her heels. Nicolò wore a dashing yellow plastic rain-jacket. He let his hair get wet.

'Nicolò thought you would like to go to the little church of San Giuseppe. Not many people go there so they will be glad of us.'

'I'm surprised anyone goes there when it's so wet.'

There were certainly only a few. 'Well, always remember there were only twelve apostles,' said the Marchesa, 'but they changed the world,' and, as an acolyte came out to light the altar candles she put a hand on Pippa's arm, 'Go to the candlestand and light a candle for Miss Fullerton.'

'Angharad? In a *church*?' Pippa still in her state of recoil could not help saying.

'Particularly in a church,' and Pippa went to a stand, put in another ten-thousand-lire note and lit one of the little round lights in their blue holders.

'One day you'll be glad you did that,' said the Marchesa.

The priest came in and began, with the sparse congregation, saying the words of the Mass, centuries old, worldwide. It was a Latin Mass, as incomprehensible to Pippa as Italian except that she knew *Domine* was God.

'*Dominus vobiscum*,' said the priest.

'*Et cum spiritu tuo*,' answered the people and, as in the Frari, Pippa knew the moment of the consecration. Once again she remembered the Passion play which then had seemed to her, as it had seemed to Cynthia, simply a play but now, on this dark wet Venetian morning, it was living.

She watched the Marchesa go up to the altar, Nicolò beside her. 'I came in because of the wet,' he told her when later he took her to the theatre, but she had seen him take communion and the beginning of a wish woke in her.

When she came in late that night there was a book by her bed, a small book bound in black morocco with the thinnest paper she had seen; on it, in gold lettering was 'New Testament'. Inside was a picture card with her name; the picture card was of the Titian *Madonna Gloriosa*.

*

This short 'golden interlude', as Pippa called it afterwards, was not all bound up with the *palazzetto* and the band: there was always dancing, her true element. She knew, too, that she was dancing well. Humphrey was pleased – he and Jasper were taking rehearsals. 'I didn't know how you would be without Angharad,' Jasper told her. 'You seemed dependent on her but you are stronger, perhaps because you are free.'

The girls were easier with her. She was no longer 'Anghie's pet'. Even when she had been chosen for the Spirit of Poetry they had not been surprised: some of them were veterans and had already seen that Angharad's pushing was not all; Pippa had already been marked out. They were used to the meteoric rise – and fall – of principals, even stars, and though Pippa was young had there not been many even younger? Long ago Colonel de Basil's Ballet had had its 'baby ballerinas', Baronova and Toumanouva, who was only fourteen, yet there was a touch of awe when they were with Pippa, 'Straight from the *corps* to soloist! She must be better even than we thought.'

The climate, too, was different: the season was now, in Venice a proven success; every performance was full, bouquets for principals and favourites were presented. Pippa had several and brought the flowers back to the Marchesa. All the dancers were fêted though Maria and Callum were the most popular. Many were invited out so that Pippa's comings and goings were not as remarked – Nicolò always waited for her in the courtyard and Juliet was loyal. Pippa had tried to induce her to come to the *palazzetto* and meet the Marchesa. 'I've told her so much about you.'

'I wouldn't trespass,' said Juliet. 'I don't think I fit in with aristocracy. I'm just vulgar.' Besides, she had met a presentable young Italian of her own. 'Not like your scallywag gondolier.' Luciano Bastonello was the son of

Signor Roberto of the jewellery shop and Juliet was dating him but, 'Scallywag or not, I do like your Nicolò.'

'He isn't my Nicolò.'

'No? I tell you what,' said Juliet, 'I'll ask Luciano to take me to the Lido and hear your band and you.'

It was Nicolò who had told Juliet about the band, not Pippa. 'You are a little oyster!'

'Juliet, be one, too. Don't tell anyone here about the band or the Lido. Promise.'

It was Thursday night.

After the last curtain call Pippa raced upstairs, changed quickly – she could be quick as she did not have to take off her make-up, in fact took her make-up box with her – but as she was going out of the door, Pearl caught her by the shoulders. Pearl still had no hesitation in teasing her. 'You are in a hurry! Pippa, is he *that* nice?' The other girls gathered round her.

'It's not "he", it's "they".' Pippa tore herself free and raced down the stairs, leaving them looking after her. Gianni was waiting in the courtyard and led her proudly to the water-taxi.

As soon as she sat down he was off, expertly steering the boat in and out of the traffic until they were on the lagoon where he gathered speed, making a fast path along the waterway between the marker lights.

Pippa had been in high excitement all evening. 'You really are dancing up!' Callum had told her in the second act *pas de deux*. This was a different excitement. Though she now had what she called 'tuning-up nerves' with dancing, she had confidence too, but with the Lido it would all be strange, a new venture. Well, the band called her Pip and Pip was different from Pippa.

The fast movement, the moonlight and glistening water, the lights along their path, the water-taxi's own searchlight, its spume of wash, all added to the strangeness. A breeze had sprung up and blew in her hair. A fresh breeze. She could not wait to get ashore but at that moment Gianni stopped the boat; as it lost its impetus, it drifted, rocking on the water. Gianni came to her. He had a small closed basket and a white shawl.

'Leda she send this. She say cold on the water. Better wear this.' He put the shawl round her shoulders and opened the basket. '*Hai dieci minuti.* Ten minutes you have. *Devi mangiare.* Must eat.'

'Gianni. I'm not hungry.'

'Leda say, "*Devi mangiare.*"'

There was cold chicken and salad, a roll and butter, cherries and a bottle of wine, which Gianni uncorked and poured into a glass for her. He filled another for himself. '*Salute.* Now eat, or Leda she cry.'

'How good you all are.' Once Pippa started she ate it all then sat, warmed by the shawl, the food and wine. As Gianni started the boat again she began on the cherries, throwing the stones into the water: 'Tinker, tailor, soldier, sailor, rich man, poor man, beggarman, thief.' It came out 'sailor'. Well, a gondolier is a kind of sailor, she thought, and laughed at herself.

'*Arriviamo in un lampo* – we will be there like lightning,' said Gianni.

Gianni shut off the engine and the boat moved quietly to others moored beside the *vaporetti* quays; he made it fast, whisked Pippa ashore into a waiting car and, in a few minutes, up the drive of the great Hotel Imperiale with its fantastical Disneyland turrets and towers, its long lines of windows and its terrace blazing with light as, standing high, it looked out to sea.

They did not go into the hotel, instead down the flights of steps to the beach with its bathing tents. Somewhere up above them she could hear the band, the music throbbing as if it were calling her. 'Where . . .?' she began.

'Here,' said Gianni, stopping at what seemed to be a garden shed. 'They give for dressing room.' He opened the door and snapped on lights. It was primitive, a small table with her gloves and tights, two chairs, a rack where her dress hung, shoes on the floor, a square mirror on a wall. 'Quick, get changed.'

'Gianni. I need to go to the loo,' and as Gianni looked blank, 'Toilet.'

'Toilet is here.' He drew back a rigged-up curtain and, sure enough, there was a commode. 'Change quick,' said Gianni, 'and I take you or Nico come. He make little interval.'

When the dress was on and she was struggling with her zip, Nicolò came in panting. At once he turned her round and zipped her up, as matter-of-fact as the dressmaker. His face was flushed, his curls damp with sweat but his eyes shone with delight.

'It's going well?'

'I believe it is. Oh, Pippa *amore*, use your voice.'

'I will.'

He kissed her – That's the second time, thought Pippa – but then considered her carefully. 'A touch more rouge, more eye-shadow, the lights are very bright.' He watched until, 'That will do. It's time.'

He led her back up one flight of steps and there below the hotel terrace was the Rotonda, open to the sky, a low balustrade round it covered in flowers. It was set out with countless, it seemed to Pippa, small tables with bottles of wine and ice buckets, glasses, silver, all catching the moonlight and colours from the fairy-lights hung in the trees. People were sitting on small gilt chairs, waiters came and went; in the centre was a dance-floor with, behind it, a platform edged with flowers for the band. It had a canopy above it hung with carnival masks, model heads with powdered wigs and tricorns reminding Pippa of *The Tales of Hoffman*. The vault of sky, where the moon was almost full with a few faint stars, was above and Pippa stopped aghast.

'You never told me it would be in the open air. My voice won't be strong enough.'

'It will, of course it will.' Nicolò smiled a coaxing smile. 'And you have a mike.'

'I've never used a mike on stage before.'

'You will now. Just remember what I told you. Hold it in your hand and sing into it. Not too close, not too loud, or it will be deafening.'

'*Nicolò!*' she said in panic.

'Sing as if you were in our sitting room. I will signal you if it's too soft, too loud. Then you can sing out when you leave the mike and go down among the tables —'

'*Among the tables!* You never told me I'd have to do that.'

'I didn't know till now, but you should. In and out among them and sing. At first loud, then soft into people's ears, the band will carry you. Sing to one person then go to another. You may have to extricate yourself. All the better.'

'The better!' But the band had started and an answering thrill rang through Pippa. All at once she saw her role as Nicolò saw it. 'I will put the mike into your hand, take it from you. Now!'

The band beat a tattoo. Slowly the couples left the floor. Nicolò came on to the platform. All the young men were dressed alike in the white goldolier summer or festival clothes except that their wide collars had striped edges of gold and there were gold studs on their trouser ends. Their sashes were red. Nicolò stood on a small dais, his guitar slung ready. 'Signore, signori, ladies and gentlemen,' he called, 'I introduce to you, Pip.'

The music began and Pippa came forward into a pool of light and a little clapping. At first people still talked, wine was poured. 'Too soft,' hissed Nicolò, but already Pippa had put more power into her voice. She heard it rise clear and cool. Perhaps, singing with a microphone, people had expected a crooning voice, drawn-out words, and suddenly they were quiet but the clapping at the end was desultory. Nicolò looked anxious though he smiled at her but to Pippa it was a challenge. The next song was 'New York, New York': she took it faster than she had ever done before, whipping up the band; she was moving, swaying, freely now, and sang 'at them' as Pem had always instructed. She finished laughing. The audience laughed, too, and there were one or two cries of 'Brava!'. Next was the song Nicolò had sung when he took them on tour after dinner at Carlo's 'Un' inglesina sul Canal Grande' but sung now from the point of view of the girl who dimpled shamelessly. Straight after it came an old Venetian song when Pippa stood still, the audience still, too: she sang it as she knew she had not sung before.

'It's wonderful what an audience does for you,' Angharad had often said. Pippa was warm and confident now.

Then the light dimmed as she began the song Nicolò had written, 'Specially for you'.

> 'I think I was born, specially for you,
> And you, you too.'

She sang it to Nicolò who answered,

'I too.

I – you.'

At the end she came off the platform and walked singing among the tables, her legs in their thin glistening tights, giving a coquettish little kick when she put her knee on a chair, her hair almost brushing cheeks as she bent to sing provocatively to a face, then laughed as she eluded hands. Nothing could have been further from the Spirit of Poetry – it could have been called the Spirit of Mischief. She came back to the platform, stood swaying her hips but kept her shoulders still. 'Specially for you . . . you . . . you' and flung back her hair as she went off.

She had to come back as the applause was real now. 'For God's sake, don't curtsy,' Nicolò had told her. 'Just laugh as if you were delighted.'

She was delighted but, led by the drummer, the band started a dance tune as Nicolò came off stage with her. 'No more now. It was perfect.' He looked at her with a new respect. 'Even I was surprised but let them rest on that. I can guess they will come back tomorrow. *Grazie mille, grazie, amore.*' He gave her a quick hug. '*Molto* fun!'

XV

The euphoria went on. Next morning Pem came to Pippa after rehearsal. 'You did very well last night.'

'You were there!'

'Of course I was there.'

'I didn't see you.'

'You weren't meant to see me. We thought —'

'We?'

'Nicolò and I. We thought I might put you off. Seriously, Pippa, I think we should say you could have two vocations,' but she looked at the rehearsal room with all its familiar things, the box of rosin in the corner for dipping shoes, the light chairs, benches. They seemed, all of a sudden, doubly dear.

Juliet had shown her a newspaper cutting from that morning's *Internationale* which was printed in English and held Andrea Strozzi's review of last night's *Tales of Hoffman*.

In this gifted Company there is a young dancer, Philippa Fane who, owing to an accident to one of the dancers, unexpectedly took the part of the Muse of Poetry in *The Tales of Hoffman*. It is gratifying for Venice that she made her début as a soloist here; impeccable in technique as would be expected, I found in her that subtle 'something more' which is so rare, I rejoiced to see it.

'And he is famous in the ballet world,' said Juliet and, 'Two vocations? No, only one,' vowed Pippa.

Then Nicolò came to fetch her for lunch. She could see before he spoke that he was in high excitement and as soon as they were away from the theatre he stopped the gondola at the end of the canal, tied it and came to her. 'Pip'.

'Don't you call me that.'

'Pippa, then. Two things have happened, good things,' and, without waiting for her to ask, 'What things?' he went on: 'Last night there was an American, Mr Hyam Pearson, in the audience and he sent word by the manager that he wants to talk with me. Today he has to go to Milan – he is a big businessman – but he will be back on Saturday night. Think! He might help us. Change everything.'

'But, Nico, it's so nice as it is, for everyone.'

'It is nice. I enjoy it, but for me it is – how do you say it? – a stone to step on.'

'A stepping stone.'

'Yes. It could lead us, where? Who knows? And the other good thing is that the *Internationale* newspaper will interview you tonight.'

'Me?' Pippa was appalled. 'Oh, no!'

'It is the very top paper. Why not?'

'Because everyone will know.'

'All the better. That is what is meant.'

'It's not better for me. I might be put out of the Company.'

'Fiddlesticks!' That was the Marchesa's word. 'I hear dancers do not read newspapers except for reviews of themselves.'

'The Skinners at the *pensione* do. They would tell the girls. I'm sure Nino at the trattoria does. He would tell everyone. You see, I've been there. He knows me.'

'You need not let the *Internationale* know you are a dancer, need you?'

'N-no.'

'They can only print what you tell them.'

'They print all sorts of things that *nobody* says. They ferret things out.'

'Ferret? What is ferret?'

'A nasty little animal that digs things out and kills. Ferret out means to pry. No, Nicolò, absolutely no.'

'It is arranged. A Signorina Fazzino is coming to the dressing room to see you after the performance.'

'No.'

'Pippa, please. You only need to be careful what you say. You can talk about the band. It won't be more than half an hour.'

For her it might be for ever but no more than the Marchesa could she resist Nicolò. She could see, too, that with an important newspaper, read not only in Venice but in its English version over all Europe, it would be an enormous boost for the band and, Am I being selfish? she wondered. Surely it would not be a big eye-catching piece. Probably most people won't read it and I have had wonderful luck so far.

But it seemed her luck was running out. When she threaded her way, that night, through the tables of the Imperiale Rotonda, bestowing her favours, she found herself singing to Humphrey.

As on stage with the ballet, when a hitch or accident occurs, the dancers go straight on with their parts. Pippa did not falter a note. 'How strange that a training in ballet should help you in pop,' she said later.

'Well, both are stagecraft,' Humphrey was to point

out when she told him. Nor, at the Rotonda, did he interrupt or speak. He was with Isabelle Pascal, the young dancer, next youngest to Pippa, and he was obviously taking her for a night out in Venice and, giving them her most titillating smile – it could have been called impertinently defying – Pippa moved on, but her knees were shaking.

Then the cameras began. She had been so completely lost in the singing that she had not noticed them until the first flash came. 'You never told me. You never warned me,' she stormed at Nicolò when she came off.

'If there is an interview there has to be a photographer. They will do more in the dressing room.'

'I won't go in. I'll go home like this. Call Gianni. How dare you!' But Nicolò had propelled her in.

'Do you like Venice, Miss Pip?'

Pippa was furious but she could not be furious for long with Signorina Fazzino: she was so bubbling with warmth and interest – a young woman dressed with Italian elegance. Pippa found herself envying the beautifully cut dark blue suit with a glimpse of a white frilled shirt beneath and the dark blue court shoes, high-heeled.

'Where did you meet Nicolò?'

'In Venice. Where else?' There was still defence.

'What brought you to Venice?' A dangerous question. 'I came with friends.'

'I think not ordinary friends,' and she showed Pippa the Andrea Strozzi cutting. 'It is you, isn't it? Pip is Philippa Fane?'

Well, what does it matter now? Pippa thought wearily. Humphrey has seen me.

She was beginning to be more than tired but when she

got to bed she could not sleep and it was no surprise next morning to have Martha stop her as she came into class. 'Don't come in yet. Humphrey wants to see you.'

She had prepared her defence. 'Isn't what we do in our own time our own business? Has singing with the band ever made me late for class or rehearsal or performance? Did I dance badly? You yourself said it was good,' but, 'Don't look so belligerent,' said Humphrey. 'I just wanted to congratulate you on last night.'

'*Congratulate?* Then you're not cross?'

'Why should I be? I thought it was most enterprising of you.'

'Do you know,' Pem had told Humphrey, 'that naïve little seventeen-year-old has managed, in two weeks, to see more of the true Venice than we in all our trips here?' and, 'How did you get to know this gondolier?' Humphrey asked.

'I didn't. He knew me. He was playing the guitar at Carlo's that first night when you all took me out to dinner and we went up the Grand Canal in his gondola. Don't you remember?'

'Lucky him! You did it in style, Pippa. Your own style.' Humphrey was serious. 'No, I'm pleased as long as it doesn't go on for too long. It's all right for three days – a bit of Venetian nonsense – and it doesn't affect what I am going to say to you, in fact it strengthens it because I know now you can really act. In any case it was decided before I took Isabelle to the Imperiale. That was in the nature of a farewell.'

'Farewell?'

'Yes. Isabelle has been invited to go to Moscow as a guest artist for a year. Maybe more. Too good an offer to refuse, so after Verona she won't be with us.'

'She's not coming to Milan?'

'No, so there must be changes. By then Maurice should be well enough to dance Niklaus again.'

'I see,' said Pippa slowly, 'so Callum and I will be out.'

'Not at all. Callum will have his chance and I want you, Pippa, to pay particular attention in *The Tales of Hoffman* to Isabelle's dancing of Antonia, both tonight and in Verona. It's a thousand pities Angharad's not here but Isabelle and Jasper will help you because', Humphrey's eyes twinkled, 'I want you to dance Antonia for us in Milan.'

All through class and rehearsal Pippa could not believe it. Only when Nicolò came to fetch her after rehearsal – Our last rehearsal – did it come out into the light of day. 'Think, Nico,' she said, 'in just two weeks I have been made a soloist and now I am to dance a principal's part.'

'Tonight you are singing for me.'

'I have two performances to get through first – today's a matinée day, remember, and it's our last night. Perhaps I'd better not come,' but she was too happy to tease. 'Of course I'm coming and Humphrey's pleased. *Pleased!*'

On the way back to the *palazzetto*, 'Please, Nico,' said Pippa, 'take me the way I used to walk from the *pensione*.'

She missed her walks with Juliet – 'Well, you've gone into a different world now,' Juliet said – and 'I want to stop at my little madonna on the wall by the bridge, and tell her what has happened.'

'If she is the Madonna she already knows.'

'That's true, but I want to thank her.'

Pippa had a bouquet: it had been handed in for her at the stage door after she had left for the Imperiale. 'Somebody must like you,' teased Nicolò.

When they came to the bridge with the gold latticed shrine on its wall, he was tall enough to lay the flowers on the ledge at its foot, as, *'Grazie. Mille grazie,'* whispered Pippa. *'Grazie, bellissima Maria.'*

While she was having her lunch she told the Marchesa the news. 'In one fortnight to go from the *corps* to soloist to a principal's part. Oh, what they have done for me!'

'Not they, you,' said the Marchesa. 'Oh, I know they have trained you, helped you, but you did it. All the same, Venice seems to have done well by you.'

'I must watch Isabelle. Every step.'

'Yes but remember it is Isabelle Pascal who will be dancing that part tonight, not you. You have your own work to do, so first things first. Finish your lunch and go and snatch a little sleep. I'll call you.'

'I'll never sleep,' Pippa avowed for perhaps the dozenth time and fell asleep at once.

It was celebration night. Both the matinée and the evening performance of *The Tales of Hoffman* were sold out, the audience expectant. 'Now we'll know what they really think of us,' said Jasper.

The response was immediate, even affectionate, some of the applause tumultuous. 'Marvellous,' said Humphrey, who had so despaired before. There were flowers for almost every principal and soloist. Maria and Callum were pelted with carnations on their individual curtain calls.

Pippa knew she had been truly winning in her Spirit of Poetry solo – even Jasper was astonished. She had seen the Marchese and Marchesa in their box and danced especially for them, blowing them a kiss at her own curtain call – she had a sustained clapping. 'Well, everybody was clapping everybody tonight,' she said.

As for the barcarolle, it was encored twice which made Humphrey fidgety. 'The orchestra will be running into overtime.' At the last he did not grudge it. 'We're safely through. Thank you, everyone.'

There was a supper on the stage for all of them, the dancers, their friends, some journalists including Andrea Strozzi but, to his disappointment, not Pippa: she had had to leave at once with Gianni, who had been stamping with impatience in the theatre courtyard.

Everyone now knew where she had gone: the *Internationale* had been passed by the girls, hand to hand. 'Is that *Pippa*?'

'*Pippa*, singing at the Imperiale.'

'How did she manage it?'

'Pippa! Our sweet shy Pippa.'

'Not so shy. She looks really hot stuff.' Callum looked over their shoulders.

'Just think! To go from the Spirit of Poetry to this.'

'Well, we're supposed to be versatile,' said Juliet. 'I hope Angharad sees this. I'd like to send it to her.'

'I know what,' said Callum after supper. 'Let's all go to this Rotonda and surprise Pippa, or do we call her Pip?'

'Don't be silly,' said Pearl.

'It would be fun. Why not?'

'To begin with they probably wouldn't let us in. Secondly, it's bound to be wickedly expensive. Thirdly, it's nearly one o'clock, we shouldn't be there till half past one and Pippa's act will probably be over. Goodnight.'

'*Sei in ritardo*,' Gianni had stormed. 'You're late.'

'I couldn't help it,' said Pippa. 'Many curtain calls.'

He hustled her into the boat. As they swept towards the lagoon, 'Gianni,' she pleaded, 'I must have something to eat and drink, especially drink,' and she mocked him, '*Devi mangiare.*'

'But Nico —'

'Nico can wait.'

Unwillingly he brought the basket but the moment the wine was poured, the picnic spread, he shot away.

Nicolò was waiting in the dressing room, anxious while the band played above filling in time. 'Quick. Not a word now. Quick.' He helped her. 'Always this terrible dancing. Dancing!'

'Well, I am a dancer.' Pippa stood, refusing to move. 'If I'm so late perhaps I'd better not sing.' She was in too high a mood to be scolded by Nicolò.

'*Basta!* You will not only sing, tonight you will sing twice.'

'Say, "Please, Pippa."'

'You little bitch!' He swung her up and kissed her. Three times! counted Pippa. 'But, seriously, Pip, Mr Hyam Pearson is in the audience. Please sing to him. I'll show you where he is. Are you ready?'

Before she slipped the moonstone into its hidden place she kissed it, too.

'Had you not better take that off?'

'Never,' said Pippa. 'It's my talisman.'

The band gave her a great welcome. I feel as if I have found five brothers, Gianni, Luigi-Gigi, Piero and Alfio and . . . No, four, thought Pippa – she could not think of Nicolò as a brother. The audience welcomed her too. When she came down on the floor she went dutifully to Mr Pearson's table. He was not at all her idea of an American businessman. Surely he should have had

horn-rimmed glasses? He was big, rubicund, with silvery
hair and kind blue eyes; he had patted her hand, and in a
pause in the song said, 'That's all right, child. No need to
try and impress. I've seen what you can do. Do just that.'

When she came on for this new second appearance
there was tumultuous clapping – plaudits seemed to
belong to this night. The band was playing as she had not
heard them play before and with Nicolò she seemed to
have a magnetic thread – he did not take his eyes off her.
He and she had agreed that, for the last appearance, she
should sing the songs she had sung on the first night with,
at the end, that lingering, 'Specially for you'.

'I too . . .
And you.'

She could have sworn Nicolò meant it.

Sure enough, when Gianni came to the dressing shed
to take her home, 'Lend me your boat,' commanded
Nicolò. 'You go with the others. I am taking Pippa home
tonight.'

He did not take her home. All the way he had sung, his
songs and hers, she sometimes joining in. Once, 'You are
not too tired?'

'I'll never be tired again.'

'Nor I.'

They matched perfectly, thought Pippa, and was not
surprised when they reached the Grand Canal, that he did
not turn towards the *palazzetto* but down another familiar
way. They were going to their own *campiello*, the *campiello*
San Giuseppe, the square, the little sleeping church, the
tree, the moonlight shadows. Nicolò moored – he handled
Gianni's fast boat as if it were his own – came lightly on

board and sat beside her in the stern, putting his arm round her. Pippa felt her heart beating.

'Pippa *mia*. I think you want it. Yes?'

'Two people must want it.'

His other hand put back her hair to show her face. '*Amore*. I want it. Very much, so much I cannot wait a single second.' But she had to have a little moment of revenge.

'Suppose I'm not ready?'

'But you are!' He looked at her suspiciously. 'Why are you teasing me?'

'Because you're such a lord.' Which is why I love you, she added silently.

'If I am a lord, I order you to come here.' Swiftly he had taken the cushions from the cabin, put them on the floor boards, lain down, pulled her down beside him and begun taking of her clothes. 'Pippa *mia*, seriously you want it, don't you?'

'Yes,' but now it was coming she had a shiver of fear.

'*Cara*, you are cold.'

'No. No.'

He began gently, though his hands going over her were big and strong. Kisses followed the hands. He kissed her breasts; at first it was too much and she shied away, then, quickly wanting more, lifted them to him, kissing him back, finding his mouth, their tongues together. It grew closer, quicker, not as gentle, he was urgent and thrust.

She felt a piercing pain and cried out. 'Hush. Hush. It is all right,' and the pain was lost as pleasure flowed through her, such pleasure and glory – No wonder people give everything they can for this! She could have worshipped Nicolò, then thought was lost as she shut her eyes and gave herself up to him . . . for ever, thought Pippa.

But it was over; for a while she lay against his warmth,

then opened her eyes. The stars were the same, the moon, the little square, the church, the tree, only she was different. She would never be only Pippa again. 'I'd like to go to sleep now for a little with you,' she murmured. 'Then, Nico, let's do it again,' but he had sat up, reaching for his clothes.

'Can't we stay here like we did before, till morning?'

He did not hear, he was putting them on.

'Nico.'

'I must take you home. *Mamma mia!* It's four o'clock already and I am having breakfast with Mr Hyam Pearson.'

She made one protest. 'I can't be so quick.'

He ignored that. 'Go into the cabin. You can put your clothes on as we go along.'

At the door in the archway of the *palazzetto* before letting her in – he had the key – he was the tender happy Nicolò of the night. 'Sleep well. No classes tomorrow.' He kissed her with a lingering kiss. 'Thank you, *cara*.'

XVI

The Company was travelling to Verona by a special train. 'Which leaves at three, so plenty of time,' said the Marchesa.

Pippa was to go to the *pensione* and join the other girls for an early lunch. 'There's no Angharad to herd us now,' they said. 'We can be as adult as we like.'

There had been speculation about who would be the new ballet mistress; there was a rumour that she would be Russian, another that she was coming from New York. Pippa, though, was out of the speculation; she and the Marchesa were having a leisurely breakfast. Surely, thought Pippa, perspicacious Marcia must see something different in her, a new bloom, her radiant happiness, but the Marchesa was calmly sipping her coffee and attending to her letters.

'Did you go to Mass?'

'Yes, but I let Nicolò off for this all-important American breakfast.'

Pippa had already packed, written a 'thank you' letter to Leda, 'All the lovely little picnics. *Grazie mille*', and asked her to say goodbye to the band brotherhood, Gianni, Luigi-Gigi, Piero, Alfio. She had given Giacomo a new press photograph of herself as the Spirit of Poetry and gone to the study to the Marchese who had kissed her and said, 'We shall miss you. Come again soon.' And, 'This isn't goodbye,' the Marchesa said now. 'As Eduardo told you, we want you to come to us often, but it won't be here. We are closing the *palazzetto* and leaving Venice.'

'Leaving *Venice*!'

'Yes. Eduardo says he has had enough. We are retiring to our country estate in Tuscany. I think you would love it there: perhaps you could have a little holiday after Milan.'

'But to leave all this. What will Nicolò do without you?' Pippa got up and went to the window to hide a mist of tears.

A minute later there was a small commotion and altercation in loud Italian at the door. Giacomo appeared. '*Disgraziato!* Pardon, Signora Marchesa. It is Nicolò. He ask to speak with the signorina.' Giacomo's wrath broke. 'He want to rush in without announcement. *Disgraziato!*'

'And you have taught him such beautiful manners. It must be very important.'

'*Si.* It is.' Nicolò was in the room. 'Forgive me, Signora Marchesa, but, Pippa, you need not go away now, at least not yet. We have had an offer, *such* an offer.'

'But I have to go. I'm packed and it's Verona.'

'I know. That is why I hurry. *Il signor americano . . .*'

'Mr Pearson?'

'Yes. It seems he is impresario. He has his own corporation – he says it is well known. Every year he comes to Europe to find new bands – he likes best beginning bands like ours. He wants to make a contract and he will take us to America with beginning payment – only beginning, he says – a hundred thousand dollars.'

'A hundred thousand . . .!' Giacomo sounded as if he might faint.

'That is not so much in the pop world but there will be more, much more. We shall have our own manager. We shall tour, not only America, also London, Paris. He likes our name but it will have to be translated, The Meteors, and we are to wear our ordinary black clothes. There may very well be an album.'

'But he is . . . Is he bona fide?' Giacomo was suspicious.

'He must be. He told me to get a solicitor. I shall ask

Signor Marchese to advise, and, Pippa, it's not only for us, he wants you.'

'Me?'

'He says you are a natural. I told him I spotted you. You will sing only with our band, but you will have a separate contract, first payment, sixty thousand dollars, so, of course, with all that money you can come.'

'You mean you are asking me to go with you to America?'

'Yes. Yes, Pip.'

She let the name pass. He was so close that she could touch him and she ran a finger down his cheek. He caught the finger. 'You won't have to do any more of that dancing. What do you say?'

'Nico, don't be so quick.'

'I have to be quick.'

'Wait. I must think.'

'*Gentilissima* Marchesa,' begged Nicolò. 'Tell her your advice but advise for me.'

'This is something on which I cannot advise.' The Marchesa was very serious. 'It is between you and Pippa. Giacomo, come. We will leave them alone.'

When they had gone Pippa went out on the terrace among the roses; she walked up and down clenching her fists.

The daily grind of ballet, always striving, aching, the sweat and the tiredness, and Wolhampton . . . or this – America, Nico and singing. She loved to sing: it was carefree, enticing, yet not as enticing as Nico himself. 'Specially for you . . . and you . . . too.' She heard her voice and his.

Nico had had the wit to leave her alone for these moments but he stood leaning in the doorway, debonair and sure. Then he picked a rose, kissed it and tossed it to her. She caught it. Nico! She thought of last night and her heart seemed to leap.

Then, 'You wouldn't have to dance any more.' The thought stopped Pippa at once.

'That's impossible.' It was like a clang shattering a dream, unmistakable, and she dropped the rose.

'You don't have to dance,' he would have argued.

'Of course I have to. I didn't choose it. It chose me.'

'Pippa, that's enough.' Forcibly now he took her inside. 'There is no time for shilly-shally. What do you say?'

She could not answer at once and he shook her. 'What do you say?'

'I say no,' said Pippa.

Nicolò was aghast. 'You can't. You can*not*. I won't allow it.'

'*Allow!*' All that had happened with her dancing these last days was suddenly a path clear before Pippa and she lost her temper. 'Has it never occurred to you', said this suddenly grown-up Pippa, 'that I have a career of my own and it's beginning to be a real career? Has it never dawned on you that, in this short Venice season, I have risen from an ordinary artist to a soloist and now a principal's part? That it is my career, mine.'

'This will be a much better career. You will be rich.'

'I don't want to be rich.'

'You are so pretty when you get angry.' He had caught her. 'What you say is all very true but ask yourself, what do you really want in your heart? Ask yourself that, *amore.*'

For a moment she leaned against him. 'There is one thing', she said slowly, 'that could make me change my mind.'

'Tell me'.

'If you will still take me to America with you and I don't sing.'

He was so amazed that he let her go. 'But I'm taking you *because* you sing.'

'Not because of me?' asked Pippa sadly. 'Nico, last night —'

'Ah, last night! That was good, wasn't it? Very good, and *tesoro* – treasure – don't worry about it.'

'Worry? I'm glorying.' The words were lost in his. 'Not to worry. *Niente bambini*. No babies. No disease. I came prepared.'

'*You came prepared?*'

'*Certamente*. Of course. Always I am prepared,' he said virtuously. 'Always!' And Pippa at once had visions of other girls, perhaps many of them, of women, all sorts of women, even tourists. For a moment she tried to shut them out, hiding her face in her hands.

'What is the matter, *amore*? It isn't anything wrong. You wanted it. I don't understand.'

'It's I who didn't understand.' Pippa took her hands down. 'I understand now, perfectly.' She tried to keep her voice steady. 'Silly me!'

She took the moonstone off and dropped it on its chain into his hands. 'Thanks for the bribe.' Then she opened the door, called, 'Marcia, please,' and, when the Marchesa came, 'Marcia, would you understand if I asked Giacomo to get me a water-taxi as fast as he can? I am going to the *pensione* now.'

EPILOGUE

'From the beginning he was using you,' said Juliet on the train.

'Yes.'

'It couldn't have worked. You are a dancer, not an entertainer.'

'Yes.'

'One must be practical.'

'Of course.' Juliet was right and, though Pippa still flinched, she had to tell herself that Nicolò was right to take precautions. 'This is the twentieth century. It's you who were a romantic fool.' Part of the pain was anger at herself; 'Fool to be so upset,' but it was the 'always' that had hurt.

'And Venice', Juliet was going on, '*is* a decaying, dirty city spoiled by tourists, not at all what your grandfather said. That was rather nonsense.'

'Yes.' Then suddenly, '*Serenissima*,' said Pippa, and felt the moonstone shimmering under her shirt – the Marchesa had made her take it back. 'That was too cruel,' she had said. 'Nico was totally bewildered.'

'In any case,' said Juliet, 'it's over.'

'Yes.' Then, 'No!' said Pippa, and Juliet who had only been told what Pippa called the outside of things but had sensed there was something much deeper, put her arm around Pippa's shoulders.

'Pippa dear, it's over. It must be. Nicolò is over. Venice is over. Now it's Verona, Milan, and think what you are going to do there. You know it's over.'

171

'I only know', said Pippa, 'I shall love him and it until I die.'

'It?'

'Venice. *Serenissima.*'